c1513

Enid Blyton's
SUNSHINE
BOOK

First published 1965
Reprinted 1990

Published by Dean, an imprint of
The Hamlyn Publishing Group Limited,
Michelin House,
81 Fulham Road,
London SW3 6RB,
England

ISBN 0 603 03262 1

Printed in Italy

Enid Blyton's
SUNSHINE
BOOK

DEAN

THE ENID BLYTON TRUST
FOR CHILDREN

We hope you will enjoy this book. Please think for
a moment about those children who are too ill to
do the exciting things you and your friends do.

Help them by sending a donation, large or
small, to THE ENID BLYTON TRUST FOR CHILDREN.
The Trust will use all your gifts to help
children who are sick or handicapped and need
to be made happy and comfortable.

Please send your postal order or cheque to:
The Enid Blyton Trust for Children,
3rd Floor, New South Wales House,
15 Adam Street, Strand,
London WC2N 6AH

Thank you very much for your help.

CONTENTS

CONTENTS

Hi, Feather-Tail!

BIG-EARS the goblin was always on the look-out for anything he could take. Sometimes it was an apple off a barrow, or off somebody's tree. Sometimes it was a biscuit from the counter of Mr. Butter the grocer's and sometimes a few flowers from a garden.

He was too clever to be found out, which was a pity, because a good spanking would have done him a lot of good, and might have stopped his bad ways. But nobody ever spanked him or locked him up for a night, so Big-Ears grew worse and worse.

One day he heard the Bee-Woman telling the Goose-Woman that she had three pots of honey still left on her larder shelf.

"And that's very good for this time of year," she said. "I've usually eaten all my honey by now, even before my bees are awake in their hive. You come along to tea with me to-day, Goose-Woman, and I will open one of my pots of honey and we will enjoy it with some new bread and butter."

"Thank you," said the old Goose-Woman. "I'll bring you a sack of my goose-feathers, Bee-Woman, so that you can fill a pillow for yourself."

Now Big-Ears was very fond of honey and when he heard about the three pots that the Bee-Woman had, he felt that he really must have some.

"I know the Bee-Woman leaves her larder window open a little way," he thought. "I will wait till she and the Goose-Woman are at tea, then I will creep along and see if I can reach the opened jar. I can take some spoonfuls out without anyone knowing!"

Well, the Bee-Woman laid the tea that afternoon, and put some honey from one of her jars on to a little blue dish. She cut some new bread and butter, and put the kettle on to boil. She put some new-made ginger biscuits on a plate—and there was a very nice tea indeed, waiting for the Goose-Woman.

Pretty soon along came the Goose-Woman and knocked on the door. "Bee-Woman, I've brought the goose-feathers for you, in a big sack. Shall I leave them out here in the yard? They may blow all over the place if I bring them into the kitchen."

"Oh, thank you," said the Bee-Woman, opening the door. "Yes, leave them in the yard—just round by the wall there.

Now, do come along in. The kettle is boiling, and I've put out the honey."

Now, whilst the two old dames were sitting down, talking and enjoying their tea, Big-Ears the goblin was creeping round the house to the larder window. It was half-past five, and dark, for it was a winter's evening. Big-Ears switched his torch on and saw that the larder window was as usual, a little open. He climbed up to it and sat on the sill.

He flashed his torch in at the opening. Where was the honey? Bother—it was on the shelf farthest away from the window! He looked at the window-opening—it was really only enough to get his rather fat arm in.

Still, maybe he could reach far enough to undo the clasp of

the window and open it a bit more. So, with many wriggles and squirms, Big-Ears managed to get hold of the clasp and move it so that the window swung open a little more.

"Ah!" thought Big-Ears, pleased, "now I can wriggle right in. That's good! I'll have to be careful not to make a noise though!"

He climbed carefully in, on to the shelf below the window. He reached out across the larder for the opened pot of honey.

But suddenly he slipped, and knocked the jar on to the floor, where it broke with a crash! Big-Ears fell on top of the spilt honey, and sat down very hard indeed. He gave a yell, and the noise he made yelling and falling, and the noise of the jar smashing, made the Bee-Woman and the Goose-Woman jump with fright.

"What's that!" they cried, and sprang to their feet. "Some-one in the larder—perhaps it's the cat."

"Miaow!" said the cat indignantly, from beside the fire.

"It's not the cat!" said the Bee-Woman. "Come and see who it is. Won't I spank him!"

They rushed into the larder—but there was nobody there. Only the broken jar of honey showed that someone had been there.

"The thief climbed in at the window, and got out the same way!" cried the Goose-Woman. "Quick, come out into the yard and we may catch him."

Big-Ears had been horrified at the noise he had made. He had jumped to his feet, climbed on to the shelf, and squeezed out of the window at once. He jumped down to the ground outside—and then he hurt his ankle!

"Ooooh!" he groaned, limping badly. "I've twisted my ankle. Now I can't go very far, or very fast either. I shall be caught. What shall I do?"

He bumped into a big, soft sack that seemed to be full of

something—and at the same moment he heard the Bee-Woman and the Goose-Woman opening the back door. He knew that if he did not hide, he would be caught.

He pulled at the sack and the neck fell open. Big-Ears had no idea what was inside. He crept in and pulled the neck together just as the Bee-Woman and the Goose-Woman came running into the yard.

"Nobody here," said the Goose-Woman in disappointment, as she flashed a torch around. "No one at all. What a pity! The thief has gone."

"Well, I shall report the thief to the policeman," said the Bee-Woman, going back indoors. "The thief was after the honey—and he took plenty, too, because there's not much spilt on the floor! He must have managed to get it somehow!"

So Big-Ears had! He had sat down hard on the honey and most of it had stuck to his trousers. Honey was thick on the back of him, but he didn't know that!

He sat in the sack, wondering what all the softness was around him, for he could not see the feathers. His heart beat fast as he heard the two old dames looking for him. They did not think of looking in the sack!

When they had gone indoors again, Big-Ears crept out of the sack. He looked very funny indeed, for feathers had stuck themselves all over the honey he had sat in. He had a proper tail of feathers, stuck into the honey, which held them tightly. But Big-Ears didn't know that. How could he? It was dark, to begin with, and anyway he couldn't see the back of himself.

He crept out of the yard and went into the street. He thought he would go to a Meeting of Brownies and Goblins in the Town Hall. They were going to talk about building a nice little hospital for sick goblins. He would go and talk about it, too, and nobody would know he had been into Dame Bee's larder.

So he limped into the brightly-lighted hall. The Meeting hadn't begun. Brownies and goblins were standing about, talking together. When they saw Big-Ears, they stared hard.

"Hallo, Feather-Tail!" called somebody.

"Does it wag?" called somebody else.

Big-Ears didn't know what they meant. "Don't be silly!" he said.

"You're turning into a cock or something," said Jeeks. "Where did you buy that tail?"

"Hi, Feather-Tail!" called someone else, who had just come into the hall and caught sight of Big-Ears' curious tail.

"What *is* this silly joke?" cried Big-Ears, getting angry. He looked over his shoulder to try to see the back of himself, and then Jeeks took him and stood him in front of a mirror, pulling his feather-tail to the side so that he could see it.

"A tail!" said Big-Ears, in horror. "Who put it on me? Did *you*, Jeeks? I'll tell the policeman about you!"

"You had it on when you came into the meeting," said Jeeks, laughing. "I don't know who gave it to you."

Now everyone was round Big-Ears, and how they laughed at him.

"He's got a fine new feather-tail! Has it got a wag, Big-Ears?"

"I'm going off to the policeman," said Big-Ears, with tears

in his eyes. "I won't have a horrid joke like this played on me, I won't, I won't!"

So off he went to the police-station, and who should he see there but the Bee-Woman and the Goose-Woman, who had come to complain about the honey-robber.

"Mr. Plod!" said Big-Ears to the astonished policeman, "I've come to complain! Somebody has stuck a feather-tail on to me, and everyone is laughing at me."

"Dear me!" said Mr. Plod, in surprise, and he bent to look at it. "A tail of goose-feathers—and, bless us all, is this yellow honey they're sticking to? Yes, it is—there's honey all over your back, Big-Ears."

"WHERE DID YOU GET THAT HONEY?" said the Bee-Woman, in an awful voice.

"AND WHERE DID YOU GET THOSE GOOSE-FEATHERS?" said the Goose-Woman, in a dreadfully deep voice.

Big-Ears began to shiver and shake. Honey! Goose-feathers! What did this mean? Could he have got himself all covered with honey—and then crept into the Goose-Woman's sack of feathers?

"I don't know anything about honey—or about feathers," said Big-Ears, beginning to back out of the door. But the Bee-Woman pulled him back and swung him round.

"Here's the thief," she said to Mr. Plod. "That's my honey all right—and those are goose-feathers. He must have been

hiding in the Goose-Woman's sack. Ah, we've found him out in his tricks at last! Stick, tail, stick tight, don't let Big-Ears out of sight! Stick, tail, stick tight!"

Big-Ears gave a yell. He knew what those words meant. The Bee-Woman was putting a spell on him! Now he wouldn't be able to lose the feather-tail—he'd have to go on wearing it!

So for days after that Big-Ears had to wear a feather-tail, and he felt very miserable indeed. Everyone called out after him and laughed, for they soon knew the story of how he had got his tail.

"Hi, Feather-Tail! Can you wag?"

Big-Ears was very unhappy. He went to the Bee-Woman and begged her to take away his feather-tail.

"Now, Big-Ears, you made the tail yourself out of your own wrong-doing," said the Bee-Woman, "and it's a pity wrong-doing doesn't always show itself like that, for then we'd know who was good and who was bad. There's *one* way I can get rid of your tail for you quickly, though, if you like."

"Oh, what?" cried Big-Ears.

"Well, if you come along here each day and let me give you a good spanking, I'll soon wear the tail away," said the Bee-Woman. "After all, if you had had the spankings you ought to have had for all the wrong things you have done you wouldn't have grown this tail—so the spankings I should give you to get rid of it would be no more than you ought to have had!"

But Big-Ears ran away in horror. What—be spanked by the Bee-Woman's hard hands? No, no, no!

He still has his tail, and everyone calls out after him: "Hi, Feather-Tail! Hi, Feather-Tail!"

And one day I'm afraid he'll have to put up with some spankings in order to get rid of it. Well, they'll do him a lot of good, won't they! Poor Big-Ears!

Whatever next!

"TOMORROW the whole school is going to the Zoo, Mummy!" said Eileen, skipping into the kitchen with her school satchel. "Won't it be glorious? We've got to take sandwiches with us."

"That will be a lovely treat," said Mummy. "What time have you got to be at school?"

"At ten minutes to nine," said Eileen. "I hope I'm there on time!"

"Well, dear me, it doesn't take you more than ten minutes on your bicycle," said Mummy. "We have breakfast at eight o'clock, so you should have heaps of time."

"I think my bike's got a puncture," said Eileen. "One of the tyres keeps going down."

"Well, Daddy says it wants a new valve in one of the tyres," said Mummy. "That's all that is the matter with it. You can easily see to that yourself. Go to the bicycle shop and get a new valve. I'll give you the money. Here it is."

"I'll go after tea," said Eileen. She put the money into her pocket. A penny dropped out at once.

"I've got a hole in my pocket!" she said.

"Well, you can easily mend that," said Mummy. "I gave you a lovely little work-basket for your birthday. Get some cotton, thread a needle and mend the hole before you lose all your money."

"Oh, I'll do it presently," said Eileen.

"You are a terrible little putter-off," said Mummy. "Presently —soon—in a little while—not yet—you are always saying those words, Eileen. If a thing has to be done, why not do it *now*?"

"I'll have tea first," said Eileen. "Then I really will do all those jobs, Mummy."

She went across to the door and tripped over her shoe-lace.

"There now! You've not done up your shoe-laces again!" said Mummy. "Sometimes I think you must be the laziest little girl in the town. Do them up at once. It looks dreadful to see laces undone and trailing on the floor, and you might trip over badly and hurt yourself."

Eileen kicked off her shoes. "I'll put on my slippers," she said, too lazy even to bend down and do up her laces!

She had her tea. Afterwards Mummy went into the garden to pick some flowers. She reminded Eileen of her bicycle and

the hole in her pocket before she went. "Don't forget!" she said.

"No, Mummy. I'll go round to the bicycle shop now," said Eileen. "I'll pump my tyres up first. It will last hard long enough to reach the shop. Then I'll get the man there to put in the new valve."

As soon as Mummy was safely in the garden Eileen picked up a book. She stole upstairs. She sat on her bed and began to read. She would go to the bicycle shop soon!

Well, she didn't, of course. Six o'clock came and the shop would be shut. No good going! "Bother!" said Eileen. "How the time flies! I suppose I'd better mend that hole in my pocket now."

But before she took up her work-basket she picked up a puzzle and shook it. Could she get those three little silver balls all in their right holes? She would try.

Of course, she forgot all about mending the hole in her pocket. It was bedtime before she knew it! And there was Mummy, calling up the stairs.

"Eileen, Eileen! Where are you? Come down and fetch your supper. It's time for your bath and bed."

When Eileen was in bed she remembered her bicycle, and the hole in her pocket. Bother, bother, bother! She hadn't done them after all. Never mind—if she pumped up her bicycle tyre very hard indeed the next morning, her bike would just take her to school—and she could pump it up again when she went home at night, after the Zoo. As for the hole in her pocket, well, she must remember not to put anything in her pocket, that was all!

Next morning she awoke feeling joyful. She was going to the Zoo, hurrah! And what a lovely day it was, too, with the sun streaming in at her window. She lay and dreamed cosily for a few minutes till Mummy shouted upstairs.

"Eileen! Are you never coming? You know you have to be at school at ten to nine punctually!"

Eileen jumped out of bed in a great hurry. She hardly washed at all. She didn't clean her teeth. She gave her hair a pull with the comb, but she didn't brush it well, as she ought to have done. She didn't do up the buttons of her dress. She didn't tie her shoe-laces.

She flew downstairs as the clock struck a quarter past eight. "Late again," said Daddy, crossly. "And your hair all untidy, and your dress unbuttoned!"

Eileen said nothing. Mummy had packed her up some sandwiches, and they were waiting for her. She gulped down her tea, ate her cereal and her boiled egg, and spread some butter and marmalade on her toast.

"I'll get my bike out now and go, Mummy," she said. "Goodbye! Thank you for the sandwiches."

She fled, before Mummy could make her wash her hands or do her hair again. She unlocked the shed and took out her bicycle. Bother, bother, bother! The front tyre was flat again! Why hadn't she gone to get a new valve the evening before. Now she had to stop and pump it up!

She pumped and pumped, and at last got the tyre fairly hard. She jumped on the saddle and away she went.

But at the end of the street the tyre was quite flat again! All the air had oozed out of the faulty valve! The wheel bumped as she rode.

"*Now* I'll have to take it back home and ask Mummy for bus-money!" thought Eileen, crossly. "I shall have to hurry! The bus goes in five minutes' time and I simply must catch it."

Back she went, wheeling her bicycle. She flung it down in the garden and ran to Mummy. "Mummy! My tyre is flat. I'll have to catch the bus. Will you give me the twopence, please?"

"But didn't you take your bicycle to the shop for a new valve?" asked Mummy, in surprise, feeling for her purse. "Oh, Eileen! How naughty of you."

"Don't scold me now, there isn't time," said Eileen impatiently, holding out her hand for the money. "Thank you, Mummy. Goodbye!"

She put the pennies into her pocket and sped across the garden lawn to the front gate. That bus! She really must catch it!

But when she got to the bus-stop, and felt in her pocket for the two pennies: they weren't there. Of course they weren't! When Eileen had run across the lawn to the gate, they had fallen out of the hole in her pocket on to the grass, and she hadn't heard them.

She felt the hole and tears came into her eyes. "I forgot the hole! Oh, dear, why didn't I mend it last night? I had plenty of time. Now what shall I do? The conductor won't let me go in his bus without paying my fare!"

She stood and thought quickly. What could she do? There was no time to go home and fetch more money because the bus might be along at any moment. She would have to run to school!

"If I run all the way there without once stopping, I should just be in time," thought Eileen. "I'm a very fast runner and I can take the short cut through the fields. I'll do it yet! I'll be there in time!"

She left the bus-stop and began to run down the road. How she ran! She turned into a lane and ran down that, then she climbed a stile, and ran across a field. Then into another lane she went, panting loudly.

And then something else happened! Eileen hadn't done up her shoe-laces, and they flipped on the ground as she ran. Suddenly she trod on one and tripped. Over she went, bump, on to the ground! She fell on both knees and on her hands too. Her packet of sandwiches flew into a nearby puddle with a splash.

Eileen sat back and roared and wailed. Her knees were bleeding. Her hands were cut. Her sandwiches were spoilt.

Still crying, she got up. Perhaps if she went on running she could still get to school in time. Why, oh why, hadn't she done up her shoe-laces? First it was her bicycle tyre that stopped her—then it was the hole in her pocket—and now it was her shoe-laces! What would happen next?

Eileen tried to run but her right knee hurt, and she could

only limp slowly along. She knew she would never never be able to get to school in time to catch the motor coach that was to take all the children to the Zoo.

"I might as well go home!" wept Eileen. "Nothing's any good. Whatever I do, something horrid happens."

So she limped home, tears running down her cheek. Mummy was amazed to see her coming back.

"Whatever's the matter?" she said. "Didn't you catch the bus?"

"Mummy, things have gone all wrong this morning," wept Eileen. "First my bicycle tyre stopped me going, then the money fell out of the hole in my pocket, and then I tripped over my shoe-laces. Everything stopped me. I'm very very unlucky."

"Eileen, I'm not going to scold you," said Mummy. "You've punished yourself quite enough without my adding to it. But I must just say one thing. It wasn't your tyre, or your pocket, or your shoe-laces that are to blame. It was you yourself. You made all these things happen because you didn't do the things you ought to have done."

"I know, I know!" wailed Eileen. "I won't blame my tyre or my pocket or my laces. And oh, Mummy, I've lost the sandwiches too. They fell into a puddle."

"Now dry your eyes," said Mummy. "I've got to go out and do the shopping. You will have to be at home for the day, as all the children have gone to the Zoo. I will leave you now—and you can just do what you like, Eileen, for the whole morning."

And what did Eileen do? Can you guess?

Well, she took her bicycle to the shop and got a new valve put into her front tube. Then she could pump the tyre up hard, and it stayed hard.

When she got back home she took her work-basket and

mended that hole in her pocket, and she mended it very well too. Nothing could possibly fall out of it again.

She found some new shoe-laces, and laced her shoes up properly and tied the laces neatly into a double knot so that they could not come undone.

"There!" said Eileen, suddenly feeling very good indeed. "I've done what I ought to do—much too late, of course, but better late than never! And dear me, I'll never never put things off again. I'll go to the Zoo all right *next* time!"

I hope she will. But she'll have to wait till next year, I'm afraid!

A Country Walk in England

SPRING AND SUMMER

It's a lovely spring day and the sun is shining warmly. We'll go out into the fields and woods and see what we can find. There will be plenty to see—birds, animals, flowers, trees, insects!

Here we go, down the little lane. Plenty to see here! Look at the daisies on that sunny bank—if you can cover nine with your foot, it is spring. And what is that brilliant blue flower, opening its bright eyes everywhere? It is the bird's-eye speedwell, the germander—or, to give it yet another country name, angel's eyes.

Do you see those dainty, pure-white flowers on the bank? They have five-petalled heads, set on a thread-like stalk and this gives the flower its name—the *stitch*wort. Look at its orange-red pollen-laden stamens.

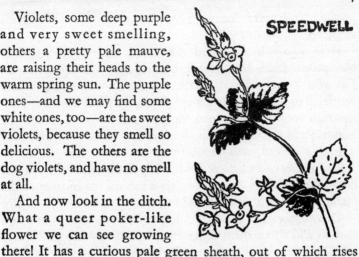

Violets, some deep purple and very sweet smelling, others a pretty pale mauve, are raising their heads to the warm spring sun. The purple ones—and we may find some white ones, too—are the sweet violets, because they smell so delicious. The others are the dog violets, and have no smell at all.

And now look in the ditch. What a queer poker-like flower we can see growing there! It has a curious pale green sheath, out of which rises a dark, purple-red "tongue". Sometimes we may find this plant with a paler "tongue" in the sheath. It is the wild arum, or, as country folk call it, "lords and ladies". The dark-tongued ones are the lords, the paler ones are the ladies. Sometimes this strange flower is called cuckoo-pint, or wake-robin.

One of the commonest plants we shall find growing in the hedge is garlic mustard, or Jack-by-the-hedge. It has large heart-shaped leaves, and clusters of white flowers and buds at the top. Crush some of the leaves in your hand— what do they smell of? Yes, garlic! Now you know why the plant is called *garlic* mustard.

Here we are, in the wood. Primroses are everywhere, their pale yellow heads rising from their rosettes of crinkled leaves. Do you know why the primrose leaves are crinkled and wrinkled in such a curious way? Well, the plant does not want the rain to run down into its growing buds—it wants the raindrops to run away to the outside; so it makes its leaves very wrinkled indeed, and turns them outwards, like a rosette. Then, when the rain comes, what happens? All the drops run down the wrinkles and drip safely away on the outside of the plant. I think that is a clever idea, don't you?

There are violets here, too, dog violets and sweet ones, and around and about them dance the wood anemones, the dainty wind flowers. In other corners the brightly polished faces of the golden celandines gleam out in a sheet of yellow. Here and there we can see the bluebell buds pushing up from their spear-like leaves. There will be a carpet of blue here very soon!

The birds are singing gaily. All round us we can hear them. The blackbird is fluting, clear and melodious. The thrush, too, has a lovely voice. We can tell his song from the blackbird's because he likes to repeat his little phrases: "How do you do it? How do you do it? *Ju-dee, ju-dee, ju-dee!*" He has a pretty speckled breast. Probably his nest is somewhere about, set in the fork of a tree. If we found it, we should see eggs there, or maybe even young birds.

The robin is singing, too, a rich, sweet carol. His nest is down in the ditch over there. It is made of moss and dead leaves, and is so well hidden in the hosts of old leaves blown into the ditch that it is almost impossible to see. What a lovely bright-red breast he has! His young ones will not have his red breast until they are grown up. Red is too dangerous a colour for young birds to wear—enemies would see it too clearly.

Can you hear the chiff-chaff? He is difficult to see as he slips in and out of the trees, but he says his name over and over again, so that you will know it—*chiff-chaff! chiff-chaff! chiff-chaff!* And now we hear another clear call—*cuckoo! cuckoo! cuckoo!* Have you seen a cuckoo? He is quite a big bird.

CHIFF-CHAFF

The cuckoo does not stay in England in the winter. Like the swallow and the martin, the swift and the nightingale, he comes to the British Isles in the spring, stays for the summer, and then is off and away again to warmer lands. We shall not find the cuckoo's nest, because neither he nor his mate make one. They put their eggs into the nests of other birds, who bring up the cuckoo nestlings as their own.

The swallows twitter sweetly in the sky. The martins are there, too, and the long-tailed sickle-winged swift, sooty-black and graceful. Can you see them all swooping, gliding, soaring, in the soft blue sky? They are chasing the insects there, and swallow millions a day. They are built for living their lives in the air, not in the trees, and when they come to ground they are clumsy and awkward.

There is another bird high in the sky, singing loudly and happily. It is so high that it is almost a speck, and its song comes dropping to earth, loud and sweet. It is the skylark, a bird that likes to sing as high up in the sky as it can fly. Its nest is down in a field somewhere, perhaps in the hoofprint of a horse.

Away in the trees we can see big black birds busy at their

nests. They are the rooks, who like to live together in a colony. They have their rookery in the high branches of the trees, and even as early as February we may see them having a look at their old nests, wondering if they can repair them, or whether it would be better to build new ones. Now they have eggs in them, and perhaps young birds. "*Caw-caw!*" they say solemnly to one another. "This is a busy time for us, with so many mouths to feed. *Caw-caw!*"

The starlings are dressed in their bright spring plumage of purple and green. The cock sparrows, busy with their nests in the roof gutter, have put on their little black bibs. Did you know that the cock sparrows, but not the hens, wear black bibs under their chins? That is how you can tell one from the other in the springtime.

Let us go and have a look at the old pond. It is sure to be full of life now. A little while ago the frogs went there and laid their eggs in masses of jelly. Now the jelly has dissolved in the water and the eggs have hatched out into tiny black tadpoles, wriggling about everywhere.

Why does the frog put her eggs into such queer jelly? It is because they might be eaten greedily if she didn't. Most creatures cannot gobble up the slippery jelly, so they leave it alone, and the eggs are safe.

Soon the tadpoles will grow their legs, and their tails will become shorter—they will be tiny frogs! Then, one hot, rainy summer's day, when the ditches and fields are nice and wet for them, the signal will be given—and from every pond will set forth hundreds of the tiny frogs, all eager to seek a new home for themselves in some nice ditch, where they can find caterpillars or flies for dinner.

There are newts in the pond, long-tailed creatures, some of them with orange chests; and, if we look hard, we may see the little spined stickleback, guarding his nest. It is strange that a fish should make a nest, isn't it? But this little fish makes one each year, and drives a female in to lay her eggs there for him.

It is a queer-shaped little nest, made of all the odd bits and pieces floating about in the water. The stickleback is very proud of his eggs, and guards them carefully till they hatch. How angry he is if anyone comes near! He goes scarlet with fury and chases away the enemy at once, quite ready to use his sharp spines on him. When the tiny fish are ready to go out into the world, the stickleback takes them for a ramble—but back they have to go to the nest if there is danger about!

The pond is a little world in itself. In the mud at the bottom move queer grubs—the ugly dragon-fly grub, fierce and hungry—the caddis grub whose body is so soft that he makes himself a little suit of armour, like a tube, to protect it! In the water swim the fish, the newts, and the tadpoles, and on the surface there are many kinds of insects.

Do you see the water-boatman, a clever little beetle who rows

STICKLEBACK

himself along with his legs? Then look at the water-skaters, skating about on their long legs! There are plenty of whirligig beetles, too, acting just like their name. Sometimes we may see much bigger beetles rising up to the surface to breathe— the greedy dytiscus who likes a feast of tadpoles, and the harmless great black water-beetle, who feeds only on pond-weed.

We must leave the pond and start on our homeward way. There are so many things to see that we would need a walk every day to see them all! Look at the elm trees, covered with deep red blossoms. Aren't they lovely? And here, growing in the hedge, is the golden palm. If we look, we shall see that most trees are flowering now—not only the almond trees and some of the fruit trees, but the oak and the ash, the beech, the birch and the poplars. We will look at them all closely and try to find their flowers, some of them not very showy, but all of them are beautiful.

The leafing trees are lovely in their fresh green. All the winter long the new leaves have been folded tightly and carefully in the brown buds. Now the scales of the buds have loosened and new leaves have pushed out into the sunshine, tender and fresh, making the woods and hedges springlike and lovely.

We shall see butterflies about—the large white, the orange-tip, the pretty brimstone—and at night we can watch for moths, for the warm spring weather will hatch out many of these pretty winged creatures from their chrysalids. We shall find caterpillars, too, greedily eating their food plant.

There are plenty of insects about now. We shall see bees, wasps, beetles, ants, earwigs and flies of all kinds. The prettiest little beetle is the spotted ladybird. She is much loved by the gardener, because she lays her eggs on his rose trees, and from them come the spotted grubs that eat up the greenfly pest on roses.

Young rabbits are on the hillside, playing among the cowslips. Hedgehogs take their little grey-spined youngsters to

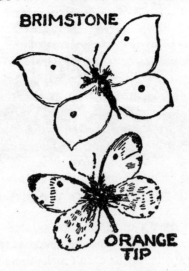

BRIMSTONE

ORANGE TIP

find slugs at night. The hares race about the fields, and the red fox watches from behind a bush. All the winter-sleepers are awake now—the lizards are basking on that sunny bank—but how quick they are to disappear when we go near. The snakes are awake, enjoying the sunshine, gliding away when they hear our footfall. The bat comes out in the evening and flutters after the beetles and flies.

It is the time for young things, for lambs on the farm, ducklings on the pond, calves in the meadow, and chicks in the yard. Everywhere there is life and liveliness, no matter where we go, and beauty in the woods and hedges and fields.

We must go now. We have seen many, many things on our walk—but there are hundreds more to see! We must go again tomorrow—and the next day and the next, sometimes with friends who can tell us what to look for, and sometimes by ourselves to see what we can find. What fun we shall have, and what a lot we shall know!

Prince Rollo's Kite

THERE was once a magician who wanted gold. He was not clever at magic, and he made very little money at selling spells, for he didn't make them very well.

But he wanted to be rich, very rich. He wanted to have sacks of gold in his cellar, and hundreds of servants round him. He wanted to wear rich silver and gold cloaks, and to have a carriage drawn by twenty black horses.

"I shall have to think of some clever idea," he thought, "that will bring me plenty of money without too much hard work."

He knew that was a bad way to get money. Nothing but good work should bring good money, but Griffin was lazy and he didn't like hard work. So he sat and thought for a long time.

But he couldn't think of anything. "I'll put on my tall hat and my grand flowing cloak, and go out walking in the field," he thought at last. "Maybe an idea will come to me then."

So out he went. He walked near the castle grounds, where the Prince and Princess of High-Up lived. Great fields lay round the castle, and in one of the fields was a small boy.

Griffin watched him. He was trying to fly a kite. His kite was yellow, and had a short tail of screwed-up papers. Griffin knew it was too short. The kite would never fly with such a short tail. It would simply dive down all the time.

Then he suddenly saw that the small boy was the little Prince Rollo, son of the rich Prince and Princess of High-Up. What was he doing there in the fields alone? He always had some servant with him to guard him—but to-day he was quite alone.

It was then that Griffin's idea came to him. "Of course," he thought, "if only I could capture the little prince and hide him away somewhere, the Prince and Princess would offer a very large sum of money for him! How marvellous! I should get my cellars full of gold without doing a stroke of work."

He looked about cautiously and saw that there were no servants about at all. The little prince was quite alone. Griffin went up to him, smiling a kind smile.

"Little Prince Rollo," he said, "your kite hasn't a long enough tail! That's why it won't fly on this windy day. Poor child, it's disappointing for you!"

"I'll go back to the castle and make a longer tail," said Prince Rollo, not at all liking the look of the tall magician.

"Oh, don't bother to do that," said the magician. "Come with me. My house is just over there, look—and I will make you a tail with magic in it for your kite. Then it will fly marvellously, and tug at the string like a live thing."

"I should like that," said Rollo. "All right, I'll come with you for a few minutes, if you'll make a new tail. I mustn't be long, though, because no one knows I have stolen out by myself to fly my kite, and I'm sure to be missed soon."

"Hurry, then!" said Griffin. "Look, come under my cloak and walk there—then if we meet anyone no one will know where you are."

So Rollo was wrapped about in the big flowing cloak and whisked off to the magician's house without anyone knowing. But once there, Griffin became very different. He locked the doors and put the shutters over the windows. "Why do you do that?" asked Rollo, in alarm.

"Because you are my little prisoner now!" said Griffin. "Aha! I'll get plenty of money for you from your anxious father and mother."

"What a hateful trick!" cried Rollo. "I'll not let you do that! I'll fight you!"

He dropped his kite and rushed at Griffin. But the magician muttered a few magic words and disappeared into thin air. Rollo couldn't fight someone he couldn't see.

"Coward!" he called. "You're a coward! Come and fight! I'm smaller than you are. You're afraid!"

Griffin boxed Rollo's ears hard. It was queer to feel hands he couldn't see. Rollo knew then that he couldn't hope to fight the magician with his hands. He must fight him with his brain! "All right," said the boy. "You win! But I warn you—if you treat me badly it will be worse for you afterwards! Treat me well, and my parents will probably be so glad that they will not try to catch you afterwards."

"You behave yourself and I'll treat you all right," said Griffin. "And don't think you can possibly escape, because you can't. To-night I shall spirit you away to a lonely hill, where I know of a tiny cottage. No one lives near it for miles."

Rollo certainly couldn't escape that day. He was locked in the one little room, whose windows were fast shuttered. There was no way out at all. He sat there gloomily, looking at his kite, and wishing he hadn't slipped out to fly it by himself.

That night the magician took him away. He spirited him off whilst he slept, so the little prince had no idea how Griffin had taken him. He thought he must have used some very powerful magic.

He awoke next morning in a small cottage set on the top of a windy hillside, sheltered by pine-trees at the back. He ran to the window. All round lay desolate country and thick woods. Not a house was to be seen!

"I should get lost if I tried to escape from here," he thought. "I wouldn't know which way to go."

Griffin seemed to read his thoughts. "Yes—it would indeed be foolish to try and escape from here," he said. "You would lose your way and starve. Better to stay here with me until your parents pay me your ransom in sacks of gold—then I will take you back in safety."

"You're a wicked fellow," said Rollo. "Wickedness is always punished in the end, always."

"Pooh," said Griffin. "Don't you believe it."

"Well, I do believe it," said Rollo. "And you'll believe it, too, some day. You'll be caught, magician, I know you will! You won't get your sacks of gold!"

But Griffin felt certain that he would, and he sent a pigeon off that very day with a message to the Prince and Princess of High-Up, to tell them that he was holding the boy Rollo for ransom. He rubbed his hands with glee as he watched the pigeon fly off into the sky, with the message tied round one of its legs.

He fed the little prince well, and gave him a warm and comfortable bed. But the boy was bored. "There's nothing for me to *do*!" he said. "Let me go and fly my kite on the hill. You brought it here with me, and I'd like to fly it."

"Very well. You can," said Griffin. "I'll watch from the window to make sure you don't try any silly tricks and run away."

Rollo took his kite out. But, just as before, it wouldn't fly properly. As soon as he got it up into the wind it dived down in circles to the ground again. It was very disappointing.

Griffin called to him: "It wants a longer tail. I told you that before."

Rollo ran in. "Well—can I make a longer tail?" he asked. "I'd like that. A really long one. Have you got any paper?"

The magician had some sheets of white paper. He gave them to Rollo.

"You tear each one in half and fold it and then tie it by the middle of the fold to the tail-string," he said. "Your kite will fly beautifully then."

Griffin didn't help Rollo. He went out into the little kitchen to use a few spells to prepare a good dinner. He knew how to conjure up pies and puddings, and that was very useful indeed.

The wind slammed the door shut. Rollo was alone. He began to tear the paper into halves. Then, with a quick glance to make sure the door was still shut, he took a pencil from his pocket. He wrote a message on the first piece of paper and then folded it and tied it firmly to the bit of string that was the kite's tail.

He did the same with the second bit and the third bit. What

did he write? He wrote: "I am the Prince Rollo. I have been captured by Griffin, the magician. I am in a small cottage on a faraway hill, with lonely country all round. There are pine-trees behind the cottage. Far, far away I can see the top of another hill, shaped like four teeth at the top. Please rescue me. Rollo."

He wrote each sentence on a different bit of paper, and tied it firmly to the tail-string. He made a very long tail indeed.

Then he sat and looked at his kite. "Suppose I set you free and you fly for miles, and someone finds you where you fall—how will they know that they must undo the papers that make your tail?" he thought. Then he took his pencil and scribbled in big letters over the kite itself. "Look well at my *beautiful* tail!"

Just as he had finished the magician came in. "Ah!" he said, "that is a better tail. Now your kite should fly beautifully. I will come and watch. But what is this you have scribbled on the kite?"

"I've put 'Look well at my *beautiful* tail!'" said Rollo, "so that all the birds the kite meets will admire it!"

"What a baby you are!" said Griffin, scornfully. "As if the birds will know or care! Come along—we'll go and fly it now and then have our meal."

They went out into the strong wind. Rollo let the kite up into the air at once. Ah, now indeed it flew well with its grand new tail to keep it steady. Higher it flew and higher and the wind pulled more and more strongly!

Rollo had a big ball of string, and he unravelled it fast. The ball grew smaller and smaller—it came to the very end!

"Hold it, hold it, or you'll lose your kite!" cried Griffin. The wind gave an extra strong pull—and took the end of the string from Rollo's fingers! Then away flew the kite into the sky, free and happy.

"You silly boy! Why didn't you hold on?" said the magician. Rollo pretended to burst into tears. He buried his face in his hands and howled loudly.

"Well, it was your own fault," said the magician. "Now your kite will fly for miles, and then, when the wind drops, it will drop too. Down to the ground it will go and some other boy will find it."

But it wasn't a boy who found the kite the next day, miles and miles away from Rollo. It was a little girl called Sukie. The kite fell into the garden, and she saw it there when she went out to play.

"Oh, what a lovely kite!" she said, and she ran to it. She stared at its face, and saw something written there.

"Look well at my *beautiful* tail!" she read. She looked at the kite's tail. It didn't seem at all beautiful to her. It was just made of strips of folded white paper.

All the same she felt that there must be some meaning in the message. She made up her mind to untie one of the tail-strips, and to her enormous surprise she read:

"I am the Prince Rollo!"

Well, everyone knew by now that the little prince had been captured, and Sukie knew at once what the message meant. With trembling hands she undid each paper-strip and soon she knew the whole story. She flew indoors to her mother to tell her.

Then what a to-do there was! The police were told, the Prince and Princess of High-up were sent for, soldiers galloped here and there, and all the people began to talk about the message the kite had brought.

"It will be easy to find the Prince," said the soldiers. "We know the hill with four teeth-like rocks at the top. From there we will hunt around to find the hill with the pine-trees and the cottage. We will soon have the little prince safe and sound!"

And so, the very day after he had set free his kite, Rollo saw a large company of soldiers riding swiftly over the lonely country that lay around the hill. Griffin heard the hooves of the horses and came to see who was galloping near.

"You can't escape!" cried Rollo. "They are surrounding the cottage. And look, they've got dogs with them—so even if you make yourself invisible they will smell you and catch you!"

So Griffin was captured, and the little prince taken home in triumph. He went to his castle, and the magician went to prison.

"What did I tell you, Griffin?" called Rollo as they parted. "Didn't I say that wickedness is always punished in the end,

always! I'm not sorry for you, because you are not sorry for your wickedness! Good-bye!"

Griffin never guessed how it was that the soldiers knew where he had hidden Rollo, and all the years he was in prison he puzzled over it. But if he could have peeped into Prince Rollo's playroom, he would soon have guessed. For there, put in a place of honour on the wall, was the kite with the message on it—and below it the tail of messages, too.

Ah, Griffin, Rollo was too clever for you, and so was Sukie, too! You should hear them laugh about you when they play together, as they do every day now.

"It's not clever to be wicked!" says Rollo, and he's right, isn't he?

An Adventurous Evening

"Now," said Uncle Desmond to his nephew and niece, "I've got to do a little shopping for your aunt. I shall leave the car here, opposite these shops, and if you like you can get out and stretch your legs till I'm ready."

"Could we go and look for some eating-chestnuts?" asked Bob. "There are some proper chestnut trees in the wood over there. Jean and I could go and fill our pockets whilst you're shopping, Uncle."

"Right. But don't you keep me waiting," said Uncle Desmond, getting out of the car. "If you do I'll drive off home without you! Now look—there's the church clock, and it strikes the hours very loudly. As soon as you hear it strike five you're to go back to the car at once."

"Yes, we will," promised Bob. He and Jean got out of the car. He looked at the clock. It said just after four. Almost an hour to find eating-chestnuts. They could surely get plenty in that time.

Uncle Desmond disappeared. Bob went over to a toy shop nearby and the two children gazed into the window.

Next to it was a jeweller's, full of flashing rings and precious stones. "Look at that ring—it's marked three hundred and fifty pounds!" said Bob. "I wouldn't have thought there was a ring in the world that was worth so much money, would you, Jean?"

"No. I'd hate to wear something that was worth so much," said Jean, pulling at Bob's arm. "Come on, Bob—let's go and hunt for chestnuts. It'll be dark soon."

They went off to the woods. The enormous chestnut trees spread their great branches over them, and on the ground were hundreds of the thickly-prickled cases. The chestnuts peeped out of them.

"They're not so big as horse chestnuts," said Bob, putting some into his pocket. "But my gracious, the cases are much more prickly! It's painful to get the chestnuts out. I wish I'd got gloves!"

They hunted hard for the biggest chestnuts they could find— and then they found that they really could not see any longer. It was getting so dark.

"It's a real November day," said Bob. "I do hope it won't

be foggy going home in the car. Come on—let's go back to the car, although it's not five o'clock yet. I can hardly see a thing in the wood now."

They went back to the car, and got in at the back. All the shops were brightly lit now, and the brightest of all was the jeweller's. The precious stones there flashed and glittered brilliantly.

"I hope uncle won't be long," said Bob, pulling a rug round him. "It's cold."

"There's not many people out shopping on this damp November night," said Jean. "Only just those two men, look!"

Two men were sauntering along up the street. One carried an oblong parcel under his arm. They came opposite the car, and then took a quick look round.

"All right, Bill," said one, and then everything happened so quickly that Bob and Jean had no time to do anything but gasp and stare in fright.

The man with the parcel slipped the covering from it and the children saw that it was a brick. He lifted it and threw it hard against the jeweller's window. There was a terrific crash, and glass splintered all over the place.

The children watched in horror. They saw the second man put his hand in at the broken window and grab a handful of rings and precious stones. Then both turned to run, as the jeweller came rushing out of his shop.

The men ran to the car where the children were, wrenched open the door, and got in. One sat in the driver's seat, the other next to him. The car was in complete darkness, so the men did not see the two scared children at the back. One started up the engine. It purred loudly. The man slipped off the hand-brake and pushed the gear handle into place, and shot off down the street, jerking the children forward.

Bob grabbed Jean and dragged her down, off the seat. He pulled a rug over them both. Jean was trembling with fright.

The car's engine made such a noise that Bob thought it would be safe to whisper in Jean's ear. "Don't be scared, Jean. I'll look after you. Don't let these men know we're here."

The car tore on down the street and rounded a corner at top speed. It went on and on, and the two children crouched uncomfortably at the back, swinging from side to side as the car raced round corners.

After what seemed a very very long time the car slowed down. It was in a very dark lane. One of the men spoke to the other.

"Better change the number-plates here, Bill. It's a pretty deserted spot."

Bill got out. "I'll leave the bag of tricks here," he said. "On the seat, Pete."

"Right," said Pete. "Buck up. I don't think we've been followed but you never know."

Bill began to tinker with the back of the car, apparently taking off the number-plate there and replacing it by a false one. He managed that all right, and then went to change the front plate.

He was so long that Pete slid down the window and called to him impatiently. "For goodness' sake hurry up. Do you want us to be here all night?"

"You'll have to come and hold this for me," called back Bill. "I can't fix it right. Come on."

Grumbling to himself Pete got out of the car. The door swung to. Very cautiously Bob took his head out of the rug, and had a look round. He could see very little indeed.

Then a brilliant idea struck him. He put his arm over the back of the seat where Bill had been sitting and groped about there. His hand closed on a small bag. In it Bill had put the rings and the precious stones.

With trembling fingers Bob drew the little bag to the back of the car. He pulled the neck open and emptied the jewels and the stones into his pocket. Then he took some of the smallest eating-chestnuts from his other pocket and put them into the bag instead!

"What are you doing?" whispered Jean.

"I've taken the jewels," whispered back Bob. "I've got them all in my pocket! I've put some little chestnuts into the bag instead!"

He replaced the bag on the seat, and then looked to the front

of the car's bonnet to see what the men were doing. They were still tinkering with the number-plate.

"Could we open the door quietly and slip out, Bob?" whispered Jean, who was simply longing to get out of the car and hide somewhere till the men had gone.

"We might be able to," said Bob, and began cautiously to turn the handle of the back door of the car. But before he could open it, Pete wrenched open the driver's door and got in. In a trice the children sank down under the rug, out of sight.

Bill got in, too. He picked up the bag from the seat and then stuffed it into his coat pocket. "What a job!" he said to Pete. "Took up quite a time."

"Fat lot of good you are at your part of the job," said Pete, in a growling voice. "If we'd been followed they'd have been on us before you'd got halfway through changing the number-plates."

Bill said no more. Bob thought he was a bit afraid of Pete. He felt afraid of him himself—he had such a hoarse, bad-tempered voice.

The car started up again, but now it went much more slowly. "Awful fog here," said Pete, impatiently. "I daren't go faster than this."

"Well, it means we shan't be traced," said Bill. "This fog will hide us well."

"Yes—but will it mean that the plane can take us off tonight or not?" said Pete. "It may not even be there, waiting for us. There may be thicker fog on the Continent, for all we know."

"Oh, it'll be there," said Bill, comfortably. He didn't seem to worry about anything. Pete growled two or three things under his breath and then fell silent.

Bob had been listening hard. An aeroplane! Had the men arranged for one to meet them somewhere, and take them off to Europe with their haul? It sounded like it. The boy began to feel even more excited. A robbery—a speeding through the night in a stolen car—and then an aeroplane secretly landed some-where to take these men off. It sounded too exciting to be true.

Jean put her cold hand in his. He squeezed it hard. Poor Jean. She was very frightened. Never mind—he would get them out of this somehow—and he'd got all the jewels safe in his pocket! Bob began to feel very clever.

The car went more and more slowly. When it came to a signpost Pete got out, switched on his torch and looked at what was painted on each arm. He got back again.

"This way to Folkestone," he said. "We're on the right road after all. I began to be afraid we weren't. Everything looks so different in this wretched fog."

"We turn off somewhere near here, don't we?" said Bill. "Off into the wilds somewhere."

"Yes," said Pete. "Mustn't miss the turning. Wish I could go fast. But this road winds so, I can't."

He drove on for some time, and then swung the car into a side road. "Now we're on the right road again," he said. "I hope that plane's arrived all right."

They went on for some time and then slowed down. The car bumped through a gateway into a field. It shook the children violently up and down. Jean gasped, and Bob nudged her at once, to keep her quiet. It would never do to give their presence away to the men now.

The car stopped. "The plane's there," said Bill, thankfully. "Good work! Get out, Pete. We can abandon the car here, and take off in the plane."

He switched off all the car lights. The children then saw a lantern shining in the field, evidently a signal. It went out as soon as the car lights were switched off. The two men got out of the car and walked across the field a little way.

"You there, Kit?" called Bill. "Ready to take off?"

"No," said a voice. "Got to wait till this fog clears a bit. It would be madness to take off now. I'd go into a hill or something."

Bill and Pete gave angry exclamations. "Can't you risk it? The country's pretty clear round here."

"I'm not risking my sweet life for you or anybody else," came the voice again. "I've only got one life and I'm hanging on to that. I'm not going up till the fog clears a bit. I think it's thinning now. Come and wait."

"We'll get out, Jean," said Bob, pushing her. "We'll find a house and tell all that's happened. If those men don't go off in the plane because of the fog, they may be caught!"

"Oh, do let's escape before they find out you've taken the jewels," said Jean, in a panic, remembering suddenly that Bob had replaced these with chestnuts. "Quick, quick, I don't want to stay here a minute longer!"

They got out of the car, closing the door quietly. They made their way to where they hoped a gateway of the field was. And then they heard a terrific shout.

"Look here! There's no jewels in this bag. Only chestnuts! We've gone and left the jewels in the car. I've picked up these chestnuts by mistake."

Bob pushed Jean into the hedge quickly. The children heard footsteps going to the car, and saw a torch flashing.

Pete and Bill had gone back to the car and were now searching for the bag of jewels.

There was a lot of growling and exclaiming as the two men hunted for the jewels. The torch was flashed all over the front

of the car, and even into the back. The children were very glad they had got out before the men came back!

"The fog's thinning, Jean," whispered Bob. "If only we could get away without being seen we could look about for a house."

"But won't the men go off in the plane if the fog thins?" said Jean.

"Not till they've found what they want to take with them," said Bob, grinning to himself. "And I've got that!"

A shout came from the direction of the plane. "Buck up! What are you doing? The fog's going now."

There was a volley of furious shouts from Pete and Bill, who were still feverishly looking everywhere in the car for the jewels. Then, as their whole attention seemed to be centred on the car, Bob gave Jean a push.

"Let's see if we can squeeze through this hedge to the other side, Jean. We'll be in a lane then and can run fast."

They managed to squeeze through. They found themselves in a dark lane, and, holding hands tightly in case they got parted from one another, the two children sped up the lane.

On and on they went. They passed a row of rounded sheds, and wondered what they were. "I expect they are something left over from the last war," said Bob. "Come on, Jean. If only we could see a house!"

They seemed to walk for miles before they saw head-lights coming towards them. A car! Good! Bob put himself boldly in the road and waved vigorously to make the car stop. Seeing a small boy in the road the driver pulled up in surprise.

"Please could you take us to the nearest police station," said Bob, pulling Jean into the car with him. "We've got something to tell the police. Something very important."

The driver switched on the light that lit the inside of the car and stared at Bob and Jean in surprise. "The police station!

What do you want to tell the police? Are you sure you want to go?"

"Yes," said Bob, clutching the jewels in his pocket tightly. He wasn't going to say a word about *those*! This motorist might be a bad man, for all he knew—and he might be robbed of them. So Bob held his tongue, and hoped that Jean would too.

"All right," said the driver, with a laugh. "I'll take you. But this is queer and no mistake. Can't you tell me anything?"

"No, I think I'd better not," said Bob. "You can come into the police station and hear it all, if you want to, though."

The nearest police station was about five miles on. The driver stopped outside and took the two children in. Jean was scared, but Bob felt excited. He had news that would surprise the police!

"Well, youngster, and what do you want to tell us?" said a police sergeant sitting at a desk.

"There's been a smash-and-grab robbery at Hailingstone, hasn't there?" began Bob.

"Well—there may have been—but that's eighty miles from here!" said the sergeant. "What's it to do with you?"

"Only this—that I've got the jewels here and I know where the stolen car is that the thieves went off in," said Bob, solemnly producing a handful of jewels. He opened his hand and the brilliant rings and stones rolled over the astonished sergeant's desk.

The car-driver gasped and so did the sergeant. He became alert at once and reached for a big note-book. He began to fire all kinds of questions at Bob.

"Hailingstone—your uncle's car—brick through jeweller's window—false number-plates—aeroplane," all the details were scribbled quickly into the note-book.

"Now—could you take us to where the car stopped, and where you saw the plane?" asked the sergeant.

"Oh no. It's dark—and the fog's still about," said Bob. "I don't know a bit the way we've come. We walked a couple of miles, I should think, before we saw the car that brought us here."

"But—we passed something queer," said Jean, suddenly. "We passed a whole lot of funny round-shaped sheds in a row. Bob said they must have been left over from the last war."

"My word—that's a useful bit of information," said the sergeant at once. "I know where those old ammunition sheds are. We'll get a couple of cars and go there. We may be lucky enough to round up the whole gang if they haven't already gone off in the plane."

"They're not likely to do that, sir, are they?" said Bob. "I mean—I've got the jewels, you see. They've only got a bag of little eating chestnuts. They won't want to carry *those* off in the plane!"

"No—you're right," said the sergeant, and he and the car-driver chuckled. "Very smart work that, youngster. Well— I'll get some men and a couple of cars. You stay here by the fire, you two. I'll get someone to bring you cocoa and cakes."

"Can't I come with you?" asked Bob, in dismay.

"Not on your life!" said the sergeant, nodding to several policemen who had just come into the room in answer to a bell he had rung. "There'll be a pretty rough house, I should think once we get to the field where those fellows are."

He gave a few sharp orders and a short explanation. Very soon two cars stood outside the station. The car-driver who had brought the children asked to be allowed to join in, and the sergeant agreed. They all set off, leaving the children sitting rather forlornly beside the big fire.

They spent some time there eating cakes and drinking hot cocoa. Then came the roar of the cars, and up drove the sergeant and his men—and out of the car also came four men, handcuffed and sullen.

"Oh—that's Pete—and that's Bill!" said Bob. "You got them then!"

"Yes. Surrounded them nicely and roped them all in," said the sergeant, cheerfully. "They didn't guess a thing. They were quarrelling about *who* had got the jewels!"

Bill and Pete suddenly caught sight of the jewels on the desk. They stared at the bright stones as if they could not believe their eyes.

"And now we'll ring up your uncle and tell him where you are and where his car is," said the sergeant. "We'll get a police car to run him down here, and he can collect his own car and you too—and hear the nice little adventure story you've got to tell him!"

Uncle Desmond duly arrived, amazed and full of admiration for his nephew and niece. "Well!" he kept saying. "I never knew I had two such brave relations. You really do deserve a reward!"

They got one! The jeweller whose jewels they had saved presented Bob and Jean with a wrist-watch each. They are very proud of them indeed.

Who would have thought that an adventure like that would have blown up out of the night so suddenly? Well —you never know, do you?

The Bad-tempered Queen

THERE was once a queen called Crotchety, and she was just like her name—as bad-tempered and spiteful as could be! She was very extravagant with the King's money, and was always flying into a temper because she couldn't have as many new dresses as she wanted to.

The King got very tired of putting right all the things that were put wrong by the Queen's bad temper. When she threw a plate at her serving-maid and broke the biggest window in the palace, *he* had to pay for it to be mended. And when she lost her temper when riding in the golden carriage and stamped a hole in the floor with her heavy foot, the poor King had to pay for a new carriage. It was very upsetting.

Ah, but one day she went too far! You shall hear about what happened.

The King was expecting some visitors from a Prince in a far-off land. The Queen was in a bad temper when he told her that they were coming, and she wouldn't have them to stay in the palace.

"It's just like you to ask visitors when the spring-cleaning is going on!" she cried. "The six spare-rooms are all upside-down, and my cook is leaving to get married. I cannot and I *will* not have visitors from a foreign country just now. So put that in your pipe and smoke it, King Bollo!"

"I don't smoke a pipe, my dear," said the King. "I should have thought you'd have known that by now."

"Oh go away!" said the Queen, stamping her foot crossly. "Go away! GO AWAY!"

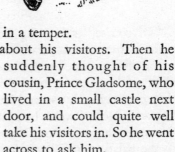

The King fled. The Queen had a big needle in her hand and he didn't want her to prick him with it. She didn't care *what* she did when she was in a temper.

He wondered what to do about his visitors. Then he

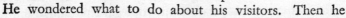

suddenly thought of his cousin, Prince Gladsome, who lived in a small castle next door, and could quite well take his visitors in. So he went across to ask him.

"Certainly, certainly," said the Prince, kindly. "I've plenty of room. They can all come and stay here. The only thing is that, as you know, I'm keeping pigs in my garden, so my grounds don't smell very nice. Could they use *your* garden, do you think?"

"Of course," said King Bollo at once. "They can come through the gate that leads from your garden to mine and can spend all their time there, if they want to. It's lovely now that all the tulips and lupins are out. Well, that's settled then—they can stay with you and have meals in your castle, so that Queen Crotchety won't be upset—and they can use my garden whenever they want to. Of course they will come to meetings in the palace, but I'll see that they all wipe their feet, and I don't think they will make much mess."

So it was all very nicely arranged. King Bollo didn't tell the Queen anything about it. He was afraid she might fly into a temper again over something and be rude to his visitors when they came to meetings in his palace.

The King gave orders to his gardeners to get the garden looking as nice as possible.

"And you'd better paint all the garden seats," he said. "They look a bit faded. Paint them a nice bright green."

So the gardeners were soon very busy. They hadn't quite finished their work when the visitors arrived, but the garden was looking lovely in the sunshine. There were only three garden seats left to paint, and these the gardeners packed away in a little hidden spot by the round lily pond, hoping to finish them the next day.

The visitors didn't at all mind staying with the Prince instead of with the King. They had heard of Queen Crotchety's bad temper, and hadn't very much looked forward to staying in her palace.

"But pray use the palace gardens to sit in and walk in," said the King to the visitors, when he welcomed them. "The pigs are not very pleasant company in my cousin's gardens, and the flowers are really lovely in mine."

The twelve little foreigners bowed low. They had come to make an important treaty with King Bollo, and they thought him a very charming man.

The next day was a sunny, warm day. The twelve visitors had a splendid breakfast with the Prince, and then they thought they would go and sit in the palace gardens next-door. So off they went, and were soon looking at all the rows of red and yellow tulips, the blue and white lupins and the little button-daisies trimming the edge of each border.

Soon they found themselves by the round lily pond. The gardeners had just finished painting the three seats there, and had left them in the sun to dry. The visitors had no idea that the paint was wet, and they sat down on the seats to rest and look at the lilies on the water.

Now it so happened that just at that moment the Queen came by, on her way to pick some gooseberries from the bushes at the bottom of the garden. She saw the twelve little men sitting by the pond and stared at them in surprise.

She had her crown on, so the visitors knew that she was the Queen. They all tried to stand up and bow—but, alas for them, they had stuck to the wet paint on the seats, and they could not move!

"Where are your manners?" cried the Queen angrily. "Get up and bow! And what are you doing here, I should like to know! I don't know you! You are not staying at my palace! Therefore you must be trespassing in my gardens. How dare you! How dare you, I say!"

The poor little visitors were frightened and dismayed. The chief of them tried to get up once more, but he could feel his trousers being torn, so he gave up trying. He opened his mouth to explain matters to the Queen, but as he spoke in his own language, which the Queen couldn't understand at all, it didn't make things much better!

"Oojatillynomkejopupillaterons!" said the little man politely.

"What nonsense are you talking?" said the Queen, stamping

her foot. "Say something I can understand, or I'll have you put in prison."

"Tippyunnyretudanelilliponotoff!" cried all the visitors in horror.

"All right, all right," said the Queen, a fearful frown on her face. "Hey! Gardeners! Where are you! Come and lock up these nasty little people at once!"

Up ran all the gardeners, and to the visitors' great horror they found themselves roughly seized. The Queen stalked off in fury, and left them.

The gardeners soon discovered that the twelve little foreigners were stuck fast to the three garden seats. So they hoisted up the seats on their shoulders and soon carried them off that way. They locked up the twelve men in a big barn at the end of the grounds and left them there until they got further orders from the Queen.

Queen Crotchety went to pick her gooseberries and they were so ripe and juicy that she began to feel happy again, and soon she forgot all about the little men she had sent to be locked up. She filled her basket and went back to the palace to see that the new cook was cooking the lunch properly.

Meanwhile the King was feeling very puzzled. He had been expecting his twelve visitors to come to a meeting at the palace at twelve o'clock and none of them had arrived! So he thought he would go to his cousin the Prince's castle after lunch and see what had happened to them. Perhaps they had mistaken the time!

But when he got to the castle he found the Prince even more puzzled than he was—for though the Prince had prepared a perfectly magnificent lunch for his visitors, not one of them had turned up! He had thought that maybe the meeting at the palace had gone on a long time—but when he heard from the

King that there had been no meeting, he was more surprised than ever.

"Wherever can they be?" he asked. "Do you suppose they've gone back to their own country?"

"I hope not," said the King, looking worried. "We haven't done anything about that treaty yet, and if they go back without signing it, my country will lose a lot of money."

"Well, we must hope they'll turn up," said the Prince. "You'd better go back to the palace to see if they are there."

So back went the King, only to find no visitors at all, of course. Instead he found the Queen waiting for him, with a frown on her forehead. She had just remembered the twelve little men she had seen sitting on the seats, and who, she thought, had been so rude to her. She wanted to have them punished.

"Some nasty little men were very rude to me this morning," she began. "They must be punished."

"Dear me, what did they do?" asked the King, quite interested to hear that anyone had been brave enough to be rude to Queen Crotchety.

"They wouldn't bow to me, and talked a lot of rubbish when I asked them what they were doing in my garden," said the Queen. "So they are all locked up."

"Quite right," said the King. "I'll give orders to have them brought before me, and I dare say I'll have their heads chopped off."

So his servants were sent to bring the prisoners, and the King sat on his throne, looking very important indeed. He didn't *really* mean to have anyone's head chopped off, but it sounded very fierce. So just as his servants were coming back, he cried out in a loud voice: "Yes, I'll have all their heads chopped off!"

The poor little visitors were terrified when they heard this. They were still stuck tightly to the garden seats, and the footmen had to carry in seats and all. They put them down in front of the King.

"What's all this, what's all this?" he cried, jumping up from his throne. "Why, dear me, these are my visitors, the little men from Far-off Land, come to sign a most important treaty! What are they doing on those seats? Surely, surely, these are not the people you complained of, my dear Queen?"

"Well, that's just what they are then!" snapped the Queen. "Off with their heads!"

The twelve little men shrieked with fear and tried to leap off the seats. But they couldn't.

"Gently, now, gently," said the King to the Queen. "I want to get to the bottom of this. First of all, why are these men brought in on garden seats? Why are they not allowed to walk in on their own legs?"

"It's wet paint, Your Highness," said one of the footmen, showing his fingers all stained with green where he had carried the garden seat. "The poor creatures can't get up!"

"So *that's* why they didn't get up and bow to you this morning!" said the King to Queen Crotchety. "They were stuck to the wet paint and couldn't. Oh, what a mess and a muddle you've made, my dear! These are twelve important visitors of mine, and they are staying with the Prince next door, because of the spring-cleaning in the palace. And you go and have them locked up!"

"Rilltobabaranurituberfids!" shouted the biggest visitor in an angry voice. The King understood the language perfectly, but the Queen didn't.

"Quite, quite!" he said. But the Queen snorted.

"Well! That's the sort of silly nonsense they spoke to me this morning!" she cried.

"Well, I am sorry to say that you have offended these poor men," said King Bollo to the Queen. "They are honoured visitors of mine, and you've had them locked up and they heard me saying I'd have their heads cut off. Now we're in a pretty pickle. I expect their country will go to war with us. And you know what *that* means, don't you? No money for any dresses or hats or necklaces! That will teach you not to lose your temper and interfere in things that don't concern you!"

The King looked so fierce that for once the Queen turned pale.

"W-w-w-w-w-what can we do?" she said. "I don't want war. Ask them what we can do to make up for my mistake."

The King spoke to the twelve little men, and they answered him.

"What did they say?" asked the Queen.

"They said that if I gave orders for you to be put into prison and kept there for as long as you lost your temper, they would forgive the way they had been treated," said the King.

"Oh!" screamed the Queen, in a rage. "Put me into prison! Oh, I never heard of such a thing!"

"Now there you go, losing your temper again," said the King. "I'm sorry, my dear, but I can't afford to go to war just at present—so I'm afraid you'll have to go to prison for a bit at any rate—just while my visitors are here. Then they can stay in the palace instead of next door, and I can treat them as grandly as I like without you complaining all the time. Footmen, take the Queen away!"

And off she went! Then what a fine time the King and his visitors had! He gave them fine new clothes, embroidered in gold and silver, and the best of meals. The new cook did her best, and the footmen fell over themselves in their hurry to wait on the twelve visitors.

The treaty was signed and the visitors returned to their own country without even saying good-bye to the Queen.

"You pop her into prison every time she loses her temper!" said the chief visitor. And the King really thought he would. But, you know, he never needed to again—for Queen Crotchety had had such a shock that she never once scolded or grumbled after that, but grew into the kindest, nicest old lady you ever saw. As for the garden seats, they were put back by the round pond—but the Queen could never bear to sit there, and I don't wonder either, do you?

IT'S RAINING

It's raining!
The fish leap out of the pond in glee,
The frogs thrust up their heads to see,
The ducks are as happy as ducks can be,
It's raining!
The blackbird opens and shuts his bill,
The robin flies through the rain with a trill,
The starlings bathe as the puddles fill,
It's raining!
The grass is drinking long and deep,
The flowers wake from their drowsy sleep
And out from the ivy the wet snails creep,
It's raining!
The raindrops sink in the thirsty ground,
And hang from the dry leaves, glistening, round,
The world is full of a gurgling sound,
It's raining!

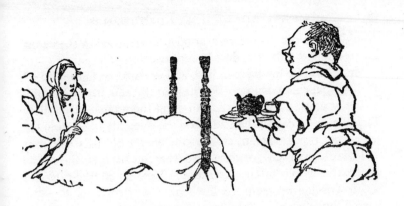

Well, Really, Mrs. Twiddle

ONCE Mrs. Twiddle had a cold and Mr. Twiddle made her stay in bed.

"But I don't want to stay in bed," said Mrs. Twiddle. "You'll do all kinds of silly things, Twiddle, if I'm not downstairs to see you don't!"

"Indeed I shan't!" said Twiddle, crossly. "Now just you lie quietly in bed and get rid of your cold. I'll do *every*thing! You just tell me what you want done."

"Well—we'll have some fish for our supper tonight," said Mrs. Twiddle. "You can fetch it from the fish-shop, I ordered it yesterday. Do you think you can possibly boil it for our supper, Twiddle?"

"Of course," said Twiddle. "Just put it into boiling water—what's easier than that? Do you want anything else fetched when I'm out, wife?"

"Yes. You can call at the cobbler's and ask him if my shoe is done," said Mrs. Twiddle. "It's one of my nice white shoes. The heel came off, and the cobbler said he could put it on for me."

"I'll fetch that too," said Twiddle. He patted his wife's

shoulder. "Now you have a good rest and I'll do anything! I'll sweep and mop and dust beautifully."

Mrs. Twiddle lay back in bed, and listened to the sound of Twiddle working below. By the crashes and bangs he was certainly working very hard. An extra loud crash made Mrs. Twiddle quite certain he had knocked over the little table on which her precious plant stood. She nearly got up to see.

Twiddle worked so very hard that morning that he fell asleep the whole of the afternoon. Mrs. Twiddle heard his snores coming up from the kitchen. She tried to go to sleep herself, but she couldn't because she was wondering if Twiddle had fed the cat, and fetched the fish, and got her shoe for her.

Twiddle woke up with a jump just about tea-time. "Goodness me!" he said, as the clock struck four. "I must put the kettle on for tea! And I haven't been for the fish or the shoe!

He took up Mrs. Twiddle's tea, and then hurried downstairs again. He must certainly fetch the fish before the shop closed, or there would be no supper!

He put on his hat and coat, for it was cold. It was getting dark too, as he hurried down the street. He got to the fish-shop and asked for Mrs. Twiddle's fish. The fishmonger picked up a nice white piece and wrapped it up in newspaper for Twiddle. Twiddle paid him and rushed off to the shoe-shop.

The cobbler had the shoe ready. He wrapped it up for Twiddle, and asked for a shilling. Twiddle paid him and hurried home with the two parcels. He was just in time to hear Mrs. Twiddle calling down to him.

"Twiddle! Twiddle! Have you gone to sleep again? I've been calling you for ages!"

Twiddle went to fetch Mrs. Twiddle's tea-tray. "No, dear. I've just been busy," he said.

"I suppose you've forgotten to fetch the fish!" said Mrs. Twiddle, who was now feeling cross and miserable with her cold.

"Of course I haven't forgotten!" said Twiddle, offended. "They're downstairs in the kitchen."

"Oh, Twiddle, don't let the cat get the fish!" said Mrs. Twiddle. "Do put it into the larder till you cook it—and bring my shoe up here and put it into my wardrobe for me."

"The cat won't get the fish. I'll look out for that," said Twiddle. "I never did like that cat of yours, wife, and you may be sure I won't let it steal our fish! Now don't you worry."

Twiddle went down and looked at the two packages on the kitchen table. The cat was sitting underneath, looking very innocent. Twiddle knew that look. It usually meant that the cat was going to steal something.

He picked up one of the parcels, opened the larder door and popped it on the shelf. "Ha!" he said to the cat. "You thought you were going to have that fish, did you? Well, think again!"

The cat said nothing. It began to wash its face very carefully, and took no notice of Twiddle at all. He went upstairs with the other parcel, and popped it into his wife's wardrobe. "There!" he said. "The fish is in the larder and the shoe is in your wardrobe. You don't need to worry about anything at all!"

But gracious goodness, Twiddle was quite wrong! The shoe was in the larder and the fish was in the wardrobe! Both parcels had been wrapped in newspaper and were much the same size. Dear old Twiddle had made a mistake as usual.

The cat knew he had. It soon came upstairs after the fish. It began to sniff round the bedroom. Mrs. Twiddle called Twiddle.

"Twiddle! Come and take the cat out, please."

Twiddle came and shooed the cat out. But in half a minute it was back again, sniffing round. Mrs. Twiddle called again.

"Twiddle! The cat's back again. Put it outside. I don't feel well enough to have it wandering round my room."

"That cat!" muttered Twiddle, who was trying to read the newspaper downstairs. He came up, picked up the cat crossly, and took it downstairs. He put it outside the door. But in a minute he heard Mrs. Twiddle's voice again.

"Oh, Twiddle! The cat's jumped in at the window! I simply can't think why she's behaving like this. Anyone would think there was a mouse in my bedroom."

Twiddle shooed the cat out again, and shut the bedroom window and the door too. "Now!" he said to the cat, "I'm not having any more nonsense from *you*! You'll just stay out of that room!"

The cat curled itself up on the mat by the bedroom door and lay there, not taking any notice of Twiddle at all. Twiddle thought it was a very rude cat. He went downstairs again, but just as he was halfway down, Mrs. Twiddle called to him.

"Twiddle, get a pan of boiling water and boil the fish for our supper. Now don't forget! And do some potatoes too."

"I was going to," said Twiddle. He soon had some boiling water and went to the larder to get the fish. He picked up the paper parcel there and took it to the pan. He shook the contents into the boiling water. The white shoe slid in, and dear old Twiddle thought it was the white piece of fish he had bought. He put the lid on the pan.

"There!" he said. "Now boil away, fish, and make us a nice supper."

Now just about then Mrs. Twiddle began to smell a strong smell of fish. "Funny!" she thought. "The door's shut, and I can smell that fish cooking all the way up here and through the shut door too. Dear me, I hope the fishmonger hasn't given Twiddle a bad piece. It really does smell very strong."

She opened the bedroom door to sniff down the stairs. But she couldn't smell the fish-smell there at all. So she went back to bed, rather puzzled.

The cat slipped in as soon as she opened the door. It went to the wardrobe and scraped at it. The door swung open a little way and the cat squeezed in, sniffing happily.

It soon scrabbled at the fish-wrapping and got the paper off. Then it settled down contentedly to eat the fish. A very strong fish-smell came into the bedroom at once.

Mrs. Twiddle heard the cat in the wardrobe and was cross. "That cat must think there's a mouse in there!" she thought. "I just can't keep it out of the bedroom! Oh dear—there's that dreadful fishy smell again. I'm quite sure Twiddle bought a bad piece!"

She got out of bed and shooed the cat out of the wardrobe. Then she put on her dressing-gown and went downstairs. She felt she really *must* find out if the fish was bad.

Twiddle was most surprised to see her. He was sitting in his chair by the fire, his feet up on the mantelpiece, reading his paper in peace. The pan of boiling water bubbled on the stove in the scullery.

"Twiddle—don't you think that fish you're cooking smells bad?" said Mrs. Twiddle. "I can smell it all the way up in my bedroom!" Twiddle sniffed hard. There was absolutely no smell of fish at all in the kitchen. "You're imagining things, wife," he said. "I can't smell any fish at all."

Mrs. Twiddle hated to be told that she imagined things. She sniffed very hard indeed—and then she sniffed again. It was queer, but she couldn't seem to smell fish at all now. She sniffed and sniffed.

"Are you sniffing to smell the fish or because you've got a cold?" asked Twiddle. "I can lend you a hanky if you like."

"Don't be annoying, Twiddle," said Mrs. Twiddle and she went into the scullery. She took the lid off the pan and looked inside. She saw something long and white there, boiling away for all it was worth. She sniffed again. There was no smell at all. She simply couldn't understand it.

She took a fork and poked it into the pan. The fish seemed as tough as leather! She poked it again, and then gave such a scream that Twiddle jumped to his feet in alarm.

"What's the matter?" he cried. "Do you feel bad?"

"Twiddle—oh, Twiddle—just *look* what you're cooking!" cried Mrs. Twiddle, and she lifted out her boiled white shoe with the fork. "Oh, you bad, stupid man—you've been cooking my shoe for supper! Oh, how *could* you do such a thing!"

"But—but I put the fish in to boil!" said poor Twiddle, staring at the dripping shoe. "And you said you *smelt* fish, wife! What's happened?"

"Where is the fish?" demanded Mrs. Twiddle, looking red and angry. "Now what have you done with that? Where is it?"

"I don't know," said Twiddle—and at that very moment they heard a noise on the stairs. The cat, feeling rather lonely, had decided to finish her meal downstairs and was dragging the fish down, step by step, bringing a very strong smell with it.

Mrs. Twiddle gave another scream and darted to the door. She pointed to the stairs. "There's the fish! No wonder that cat's been in my bedroom half the time. It smelt the fish there. You put it into my wardrobe, and you put my shoe into the pan to boil. What have you got to say to *that*, Twiddle?"

Twiddle felt that he had a lot to say about the cat, but he thought he'd better not. He patted his cross little wife, and tried to make her go to bed again.

"I'll bring up your supper soon. You go back to bed," he said.

"I don't want cooked shoe!" said Mrs. Twiddle, bursting into tears.

"No—it's that cat who ought to be cooked!" said Mr. Twiddle under his breath. "Shoo, Puss, shoo!"

"Don't *mention* the word 'shoe' to me or the cat!" wept Mrs. Twiddle. "I'll have a boiled egg for my supper—but I know I shan't get it. You'll cook a couple of boots instead!"

Poor Twiddle. He's a terrible fellow for making mistakes, isn't he?

SPRING HERALDS

Blow your trumpets, daffodils,
    For Spring is coming now,
Shake out your pretty golden frills,
    And make a little bow!
Small heralds of the Spring are you,
    Dressed in suits of gold,
Dancing gaily all day through
    In the breezes cold.

Tan-tara! The trumpets sound
    True and sweet and clear;
Daffies, curtsy to the ground,
    For Spring, yes Spring is here!

Santa Claus is Surprising

IT WAS December, and the schoolchildren were beginning to think of decorating their schoolroom and making their Christmas cards. In Miss Brown's class there were thirty-two boys and girls, and they were all getting excited.

"Do you know what *I'm* going to have for Christmas?" boasted Tom. "I'm having a new bicycle, with a bell and a pump and a lamp."

"And I'm having a big doll's cot," said Prue. "I've got one already, but want another. I've written a letter to Santa Claus, and told him all the other things I want as well."

"I want a new engine," said Dan. "And I want a big set of railway lines, too, and a tunnel and a station. My dad says they cost a lot, but I guess he'll get them for me."

Miss Brown listened to the children talking to one another. "Now this is all very interesting," she said, "but let's talk now of what *you* are planning to give your relations and friends. Prue, what are you going to give your mother?"

"Oh—she won't expect more than a card," said Prue. "I shan't buy her anything."

"But you have so much money given to you each week, Prue," said Miss Brown, shocked. "Can't you even buy your mother some flowers? She would be so pleased."

"Well, I go to the pictures twice a week, and I like to buy myself sweets to eat there," said Prue. "That takes up nearly all my money. Mother's got everything she wants. Why should I buy her something else?"

"It's too much bother to think what people want," said Tom. "I shall give my little brother a shilling, and let him get what he likes. That is, if I still have a shilling after I've bought the things I want myself."

"The trouble is," said Miss Brown, "you all have too much money now, and too many things, and it has made you selfish, so that you can't even be bothered to think of other people and plan for them at Christmas time."

"*I* don't have much money," said Eileen's small voice. "We're ten in our family, and we don't get many things. But

I've saved up sixpence, and I'm going to buy my mother a little pot-plant. She loves them."

"I'm glad, Eileen," said Miss Brown. "I suppose you've asked Santa Claus for a whole list of things, though, just like everyone else."

"No, I didn't," said Eileen. "There are ten of us asking him for things, so we've each asked for only one. My mother said that would be fairest."

"You have a good and sensible mother, then," said Miss Brown. She looked a bit sad. She liked her boys and girls so much, but somehow they didn't seem as nice as they used to be. She remembered how they used to plan for Christmas, and make out lists of things they wanted to buy for their mothers and fathers, and brothers and sisters, and how they used to go without sweets and treats to save up their money to go and shop at Christmas-time.

"We used to have fun," she said, half to herself. "I remember little Lily Jones—how she saved up all the ha'pennies she got for running errands, and bought her grandmother, who was ill, a red cushion for her old chair. And I remember how Lily brought the cushion proudly to school, and all the boys and girls sat on it one by one to feel how soft it was. And I remember how one year the boys saved up enough pennies to buy one of their little friends in hospital the favourite book she wanted at Christmas-time. How pleased and proud they were when we decided that three of them should go to the hospital and present the book to Mary, with flowers from all of us."

The children listened. They always liked Miss Brown's memories about other boys and girls she had had in her class.

"Tell us some more," said Eileen.

"No. You're not the same kind of children any more, most of you," said Miss Brown. "You expect so much and you give so little, and that is all wrong. But I'm afraid I can't alter you.

It's such fun to save up for others, and to give them pleasure—but you think it's too much bother to do that now."

"Are we going to have the usual Christmas party this year?" asked Tom. "You know—with balloons and crackers, and sweets and presents off the Christmas tree?"

"And will Santa Claus come to it as he usually does?" called out one of the small ones. "I want him to come."

Now, the Santa Claus at Miss Brown's Christmas party was always her big, burly brother, as most of the children knew. They loved him. He had a fine, hearty voice, twinkling blue eyes and could make wonderful jokes. He knew all the children's names, and gave them each a balloon, a bag of sweets, three crackers, and a big and little present off the tree.

So no wonder the children looked forward to the Christmas party. Last year they had had one, too, and it had been difficult to get enough things for the children, so Miss Brown and her brother had had to work very hard indeed to find presents that the children would like.

Miss Brown had been rather upset after the party. Only two children had come to thank her for it, and to say how kind it was of her and her brother to give them such a good time. Only two! What was happening to children nowadays? She liked them as much as ever—but something was spoiling them.

Her brother came to see her that afternoon, and they talked about the party—the one they wanted to give that Christmas.

"I suppose you'll like me to dress up as Santa Claus and come along as usual?" said Paul, her big, burly brother. "Do the children deserve a fine slap-up party? I've got a chance of getting a very good lot of toys for the tree this year."

"Oh, Paul, you know how much I love all my school-children," said Miss Brown, "but something is going wrong with such a lot of them. They are getting selfish and ill-mannered, and they won't do anything for anybody unless they are paid for it. And do you know, heaps of them this Christmas are asking for all kinds of things from their parents—and are not even bothering to buy them anything themselves, though they have lots of money."

"Disgusting," said Paul, who sometimes thought that a good spanking would put some sense into a few of the children's heads. "Well, do you expect me to act as Santa Claus to a lot of children like that? I won't! I don't mind giving up my time and money to bring pleasure to nice-natured children, but I'm not going to help to spoil bad-natured ones. No, my dear. I'm sorry, but this year I only act as Santa Claus to decent children."

"Oh, Paul," said Miss Brown. "You can't come and hand out presents to some children and not to others."

"Indeed I can," said Paul. "With much pleasure! And if you want me to hand out a present to that little bully of a Tom and that bad-tempered Prue, and that selfish Dan, you're mistaken. I shan't."

"But I shan't know which children to pick out for presents and which not," said Miss Brown. "Some of them may be better or worse than I think they are and we might make a bad mistake."

"Now look here, my dear, I'll tell you how to find out which children will deserve a treat or not," said Paul. "You take arithmetic every day, don't you? Well, one day tell the children that you want them to make out bills for themselves. They are to put down what money they have saved up for Christmas and what they have spent it on, or are going to spend it on, and for whom—then just hand all the little bills to me, with the children's names on, and I'll soon decide the matter for you. Now, I shall only come as Santa Claus this year if you do that."

"Very well," said Miss Brown. "But I'm afraid some of the children will be cross and disappointed."

"You let them try being cross with *me*," said Paul, who had a very hot temper at times. "As for being disappointed, that will be good for selfish children."

Well, Miss Brown did as her brother wanted her to, and told the children to make out Christmas bills for themselves. "Put your name at the top. Put the amount of money you have to spend. Put what you are going to spend it on, how much the things will cost, and to whom you are going to give them," she said. "That will be proper Christmas arithmetic."

The children thought that was fun. Much better than
ordinary sums! They set to work with a will. Miss Brown
collected all the sums at the end of the lesson.

She gave them to her brother when she next saw him. He
glanced at them quickly. The first one he saw was Tom's.

"Look at this," he said to his sister. "Here is Tom's
Christmas spending:

Money to spend—Sixteen shillings.

How I shall spend it:

New wheels for my scooter	..			5	0
Pictures	..	..	..	..	5	0
Sweets	..	..	..	..	5	0
Papers	..	..	..	..	1	0
				16	**0**

"Oh dear!" said Miss Brown. "Nothing for his mother,
even."

"And look at *this* selfish bill," said Paul. It was Prue's.

Money to spend for Christmas: Nine shillings and sixpence.

I shall spend it on:

Red Christmas ribbon for my hair		2	3
Pictures	..	..	..	..	3	0
Chocolate bars	..	..	..	1	6
A book I want	..	..	..	2	6
Card for Granny	..	..	..		3
			9	**6**

"Dreadful!" said Miss Brown. "Just threepence for a card for her Granny—no one else thought of at all!"

"Here's a better one!" said Paul, and he gave Miss Brown Eileen's bill.

Money to spend: a shilling.

I shall spend it like this:

Little plant for Mother	..	..	6
Pipe-cleaners for Dad	..	..	1
Peppermints for Gran	..	..	3
Sweets for the others	..	..	2

1	0

"She does more with her shilling than any of the others have done with much more money," said Paul. "Well, thank you for the bills, my dear. Now, look out for me at the party."

The day of the Christmas party came. The children flocked into the decorated schoolroom, most excited. Would there be balloons and crackers and presents on the tree? Would there be Santa Claus again?

They all sat down to a lovely tea. Miss Brown and her mother made all the cakes themselves, and they were delicious!

After tea there were games—and then came a loud banging at the front door, and a jingling of bells. "Santa Claus! Santa Claus," cried all the children in delight. And in he came, laden with balloons and boxes of crackers. The children crowded round him.

"Hallo, hallo! Merry Christmas!" boomed Santa Claus, his blue eyes twinkling. "Now, now, let me go. How can I give out crackers and balloons if you hang on like this? Now,

where's my list? I've got a list of names this year. Aha! I've only got the nice-natured children down this time, the ones that deserve a treat. Get back, all of you!"

Rather surprised, the children went back a little. How very curious—on each balloon was a tag with a name, and on each cracker, too! A balloon for Eileen, one for shy, kind little Laura, one for good-hearted Ken, one for small, merry Hilda, and one for unselfish John, who always stayed behind on Fridays to help Miss Brown clear up the handwork things. One for Teresa, who ran errands for her old Granny, and one for Peter, who was always so good at sharing his tricycle.

But only a few of the 32 children got a balloon, and only a few had crackers handed to them. "If there is no balloon or cracker with your name on, you can't have one," said Santa Claus. "No, Tom, you had sixteen shillings and you didn't spend even a penny on your mother. No balloon for you! No,

Prue, there isn't one for you, either. You only put aside three-pence for somebody else this Christmas, and you had nine shillings and sixpence."

The children were amazed. Could Santa Claus really be Miss Brown's brother this time? He knew so much! It must be the *real* Santa Claus! Some of them began to feel uncomfortable.

The bags of sweets were given out—to the same children again! Eileen was so pleased with hers.

"Ah, Eileen—I wanted to tell you that I know how you spent your money for Christmas, and I'm very proud of you!" suddenly boomed Santa Claus. "I hope your mother will like her pot-plant, and your father will like his pipe-cleaners, and——"

Eileen looked startled. Why, Santa Claus knew all about her! It *must* be the real Santa Claus. Why—he knew about everyone!

Then, suddenly, in its dark corner, the big Christmas tree

glowed brightly. Oh, the presents on it! The dolls and horses
and aeroplanes and books and engines! The children ran to it
in glee.

But again there were little labels on each toy, with the names
of children! And again they were the same names as before!
Not Tom's, not Prue's, not Dan's, not Winnie's, not Jane's
. . . only those children who had already had balloons, crackers
and sweets.

" 'Tisn't fair!" yelled Prue, angrily. Santa Claus rounded on
her at once, and his big voice boomed out loudly.

"What do you mean, it isn't fair? How dare you talk to
Santa Claus like that! Isn't it fair to reward kindness and
generosity and unselfishness and love? Isn't it fair to punish
the opposite? Well, for once in a way I'm picking out only the
right children to give my presents to. The others I'm leaving
out. And I shall do the same each year. Go
home if you think this isn't fair. AND DON'T
YOU TALK LIKE THAT AGAIN!"

Prue was a spoilt child, used to having her own way and saying what she liked. But this time she didn't care to say any more!

When the time came for the children to go home, a few of them were very happy, for they were loaded with gifts. Most of them were upset and shocked—but they couldn't help feeling that Santa Claus had been fair and just. He had treated them exactly as they had treated their families and friends.

"Poor children!" said Miss Brown to her brother. "Do you think they've learnt their lesson?"

"I don't know," said Santa Claus. "But I do hope so!"

I wish I knew whether they did learn it or not. Do *you* think they did?

EASTER GOODIES

In the shop are Easter eggs, ribbony and gay,
Made of creamy chocolate to eat on Easter Day.
(And in the hedge are Easter eggs as blue as April's sky,
The little Dunnock told me as I went running by.)
In the shop are bunnies too, with ribbons and with bows,
Balancing a chocolate egg upon their little toes.
(But on the hills are baby ones, as furry as can be,
They all come out and sit around and *how* they stare at me!)
In the shop are Easter chicks of every shape and size,
And some have little feather-wings and some have button-eyes.
(But at the farm are yellow chicks that cheep and peck and run,
I *wish* I could have one of those—wouldn't it be *fun*!)

DAFFODIL

There she dances, dressed in gold,
Whilst the March winds, frosty-cold,
Blow her gown so frilly;
Like a maiden, slim and fair,
Tossing back her golden hair,
Yellow daffodilly!

THE SAND CASTLE

I had a castle made of gold,
It stood up straight and strong and bold,
   With towers tall and square,
Its windows shone with pearly shell,
And in it, by a fairy spell,
   I put a Princess fair.

I was the giant, grim and tall,
That sat upon the castle wall
   And watched for foeman strong;
Then, riding on a sea-horse white,
With flag of seaweed shining bright,
   A Sea-Prince came along!

He brought an army clad in green,
The biggest waves I've ever seen,
   All topped with curling spray!
They battered at my castle door,
And though I fought them, hundreds more
   Came rushing to the fray!

And now, alas! My castle grand
Is just a bit of crumbling sand
   Hidden by the sea;
The Prince has saved the maiden fair,
I'm quite defeated—*I* don't care,
   I'm going home to tea!

Ring the Bell and Run Away

THERE WERE once two children who were always in mischief. Sometimes they hid around a corner and jumped out at other children. Sometimes they climbed up trees and dropped things down on passers-by underneath.

But their favourite trick was to ring someone's bell and then run away. How they loved doing that!

They rang old Mrs. Brown's bell, and the lame old lady limped to the door many times to see who was there—and nobody was.

They rang the bell at the Big House, and Mary, the busy maid, wasted a great deal of time running to the door and opening it—and there was no one there.

Sometimes they rang their school-teacher's bell, and they thought that was very daring. Miss Jones lived in a little house next to the school. She was tired at the end of the day, for she had forty-three children in her class.

Just as she had settled down to do some work for the next day, her door-bell would sound. "Ping-ing-ing-ing! Ping-ing-ing-ing!"

Up she would get—but when she opened the door, there was nobody about. How annoying when she was tired! No sooner had she sat down again than the bell rang once more. "Ping-ing-ing-ing!"

"Surely none of my children would be so unkind as to play a silly trick like this on me," thought Miss Jones. "They all know I'm tired at the end of the day."

But it *was* two of her children—Jock and Jessie, always so pleased to be into mischief of some kind.

Now one day they were sent to the farm over the hill to get some eggs.

"Bother!" said Jessie, swinging the basket as they set off. "We don't pass a single house on the way. We shan't be able to ring the bell and run away."

They went across two fields. They crossed the bridge over the stream. They went across another field, where poppies danced on their thin stalks. Then they took the path that led over Blowy Hill. It was a good name for it because a wind always blew there.

"Let's take that rabbit-path over there!" said Jessie, suddenly. "Look, it's a nice narrow little path, winding all about."

So they took the little rabbit-path—and to their great surprise, what did they come to but a small green and yellow door, set right in the side of the hill itself!

"Look at that!" said Jock, in amazement. "I never saw that before. Does somebody live in this hill? Maybe that wasn't a rabbit-path after all—it runs right up to that door. Look!"

They stood and stared at the little door. It had a very bright knocker in the shape of a mouse's head. It had a bright letter-box. And it had a fine bell, the kind you have to pull at to make it ring. The rope to ring the bell hung down beside the door, and to it was pinned a small card that said "Pull hard."

Jessie giggled. "Let's do what it says and pull hard!" she said. "Then we'll run away and hide. Come on! We'll see who lives there. We'll hide behind that bush and watch."

So they went up to the door with its shiny knocker. They pulled hard at the rope that rang the bell and at once they heard it inside the hill.

"Jing-jangle-jangle, jing-jangle-jangle!"

They shot behind the bush and waited to see who would open the door. But nobody did. How queer!

"Let's ring again," whispered Jessie. "There must be someone at home. Come on."

So they crept out from behind their bush and rang again. "Jing-jangle-jangle, jing-jangle-jangle!" went the bell, making a tremendous noise.

The children were just running behind their bush when they heard a voice that made them jump. "Why do you ring my bell?" said the voice, politely. "Did you want to speak to me? Why hide behind the bush if you want to visit me?"

The children turned and saw a brownie man, with the bluest eyes they had ever seen. He was just coming up the little path and he carried a basket in his hand. He had a long beard that was divided into two, and neatly tucked into his belt.

Jessie and Jock didn't know what to say. They went red and stood there looking rather stupid. The brownie suddenly looked very stern.

"Are your names Jessie and Jock?" he said, and his blue eyes shone like bits of April sky. "Are you the silly children who play that ringing-the-bell-and-run-away trick on people? Yes, you are! Well, you come with me, and you shall do a bit of bell-answering, instead of bell-ringing!"

Out shot his two long arms, and, leaving his basket on the ground, he took the children to his front door. He pushed it open, and

Jock and Jessie found themselves in a long, dark passage.
They all went down it, and came to some steps that seemed
to go right down into the depths of the earth! Then came
another dark, winding passage, and at last they came to a bright
and cheery little room, with a fine fire burning, and a cat and
dog lying together in front of the fire.

"Now," said the brownie, sternly. "You'll just stay here all
day long and answer my bell for me, see? It will do you good
to run and answer bells for a change! I've got to go out again
and I shan't be back till tea-time. See that you have some
bread-and-butter cut for me, and the kettle boiling on the fire.
And remember this—ANSWER THE BELL IF IT RINGS.

If Mr. Crosspatch comes, tell him I'll be back at tea-time. If the Snappy-Man comes, tell him the same. If Dame Scowl arrives, say I'll see her tomorrow."

These possible visitors didn't sound at all nice. The children felt alarmed. Jock stamped his foot and spoke angrily.

"Do you suppose we're going to stay here and answer your stupid bell? I won't!"

The dog got up and growled, showing big, white teeth. "You'll do as you're told," said the brownie, going out of the room. "If you don't Growler will have something to say to you—and maybe Purry the Cat will too!"

The cat hissed and stretched out long claws. Jessie and Jock felt afraid. They sat down, trembling, hearing the feet of the

brownie patter along down the long dark passage. Far away they heard a door slam. He had gone.

"This is horrid," said Jessie. "Shall we try and escape?"

"No. That brownie will only be waiting out there for us, I expect," said Jock, gloomily. "Hark—that's the bell."

It was. "Jing-jangle-jangle, jing-jangle-jangle!" it went, almost deafening them. Then it rang again, even more loudly.

"I don't want to go and open the door in case it's one of those horrid visitors the brownie told us about," said Jessie. "And I don't like those long, dark passages, either."

The dog went up to Jock and growled as if to say, "Go and open the door." The cat dug a claw into Jessie. She squealed.

"We shall have to answer the bell!" she said; and the two went down the dark passage, up the long flight of steps and then along the other passage to the front door.

When they opened it no one was there. Jessie slammed it. She felt cross. They walked back to the cheery little room. It seemed to the children as if both the cat and dog were smiling.

No sooner had they sat down than the bell rang again: "Jing-jangle-jangle, jing-jangle-jangle."

And again there was nobody at the door. This happened seven times, and the children began to feel tired and angry. But they had to answer the bell because if they didn't the cat and dog growled and hissed.

The eighth time it rang the two animals did nothing. They just lay peacefully in front of the fire. "Don't let's go this time," whispered Jessie. So they didn't. The bell rang again, very, very loudly. "JING-JANGLE-JANGLE! JING-JANGLE-JANGLE!"

Still they didn't answer it. Then to their horror, they heard footsteps stamping along to the room they were in, and the door flew open.

In came an extremely angry-looking man. There was no doubt at all that it was Mr. Crosspatch. He yelled at them:

"So there *was* somebody in, after all! Why didn't you answer the door? Too lazy? What you want is a jolly good shaking!"

And, to the children's dismay, he picked them up and shook them as if they were mats! How their teeth rattled! How their heads spun! Then he dropped them on the floor and stamped out.

"Ho! That will teach you to answer bells," they heard him say.

They were frightened. When the bell rang a minute later they tore off to answer it. But there was nobody at the door. How very annoying! The bell rang four times and each time there was nobody there.

They didn't answer it the next time. They felt angry. Let the bell ring. But alas! it was Mr. Snappy-Man, and he came tearing down the passages to see why nobody opened the door.

He was a little fellow, very sharp and snappy in his speaking, and with eyes that snapped in his head. "What!" he roared, jumping up and down in rage, "you were in and didn't answer the bell! I'll box your ears!"

And before poor Jock and Jessie could get out of his way he had slapped them hard on their ears. Then away he went as fast as he had come.

The children cried bitterly. When the bell rang next they didn't know whether to answer it or not. They thought they had better, so they went. But, of course, there was nobody there.

They answered it five times, and found nobody at the door; and the sixth time, when they *didn't* answer it, who should be ringing it but Dame Scowl.

And in *she* came in a very fine temper. She didn't shake them or box their ears. She spanked them, and the dog and the cat peeped out from under the couch and watched.

"I came for a cup of tea," she said, "and all I find is two children too rude and lazy to open the door when I pull the bell."

Out she went, and the children dried their eyes and looked at the clock. It struck four.

"We had better cut some bread-and-butter and put the kettle on to boil," said Jessie. So they did, feeling thankful that the door-bell didn't ring any more.

In a little while they heard footsteps coming down the passage, and in came the brownie, carrying a very full basket. He grinned at them.

"Had a nice day?" he said.

Jessie burst into tears. She told him all that had happened—how each time they had gone to the door nobody had been there, and when they *hadn't* gone it had been a cross and unpleasant visitor, who had come in and punished them.

"Too bad, too bad," said the brownie, taking some cream-cakes, jam-tarts, ginger biscuits and a jam roll out of his basket. "Still, what are you to do if bad-mannered people come and ring at your bell and run away? You simply don't know whether to open the door or not, do you?"

"No," said Jessie, going very red. "Brownie, you've just been treating us as we've treated other people, haven't you?"

"I have," said the brownie, setting out the delicious cakes

on a plate. "Not very pleasant, is it? I wonder if you've learnt your lesson? If you have, I'd be glad if you would have tea with me. I can't eat all these cakes by myself."

He smiled a very sweet smile, and his eyes shone like forget-me-nots. Jessie and Jock suddenly liked him tremendously, in spite of the trick he had played them. They smiled back.

"Yes, we've learnt our lesson," said Jock; and he pulled three chairs up to the table. "We've been awfully silly. It's horrid to play tricks as stupid as that. We'll never do it again."

"Good," said the brownie. "Well, have some bread-and-butter with a spot of home-made honeysuckle jam, and then we'll start on the cakes, and if anybody rings the bell whilst we're having tea *I'll* answer it for a change!"

But it didn't ring. Wasn't that lucky? And now Jock, Jessie and the brownie are really great friends, and see each other every week. Maybe they'll show you that green and yellow door in the hillside if you ask them.

Father Time and His Pattern Book

ONE New Year's Eve, in the middle of the night, Robin woke up with a jump. He sat up in bed and listened. Whatever could have awakened him?

Then he heard slow footsteps outside his window, and he wondered who could be wandering round the garden in the middle of the night!

"Perhaps it is someone lost in the snow," he thought. So he jumped out of bed and went to the window. He opened it and leaned out. It was dark outside, but he could just make out something moving below.

"Who's there?" he called. And a most surprising answer came up to him:

"I'm Old Father Time! I've come to collect this year's patterns."

"This year's patterns! Whatever do you mean?" said Robin in astonishment. "And what are you doing in our garden?"

"Well, I came to collect your pattern too," said the old man.

"I haven't got a pattern!" said Robin. "You must be dreaming."

"Maybe I am," said Father Time. "But my dreams are true ones. It's cold out here, little boy. Let me in and I will show you some of my patterns."

"I think there's a fire in the dining-room, if it hasn't quite gone out," said Robin, excited. "I'll let you in at the front door, and we can go into the dining-room for a bit. Shall I wake Mother?"

"Oh no," said Father Time. "Don't wake anyone. Hurry up and let me in."

Robin slipped downstairs. He opened the front door quietly and someone came in. Robin went to the dining-room and switched on the light. Then he saw his visitor for the first time.

Father Time was an old, old man. His beard almost reached the ground. He had a wise and kindly face, with dreamy, happy eyes and a sad mouth. He carried a great scythe with him, which Robin was most surprised to see.

"What's that for?" he
asked. "Did you get it out
of our gardener's shed?
It's what we use to cut the
long grass."

"This scythe is mine,"
said Father Time. "I use
it to cut away the years
from one another. I cut
time with it."

"How queer!" said
Robin, feeling excited.
"Now, do show me the
patterns you spoke about!
Where are they? And what
are they?"

Father Time didn't have
any book of patterns.
Robin had thought he
would have one rather
like the book of patterns
that Mother sometimes got
from the man who sold
them their curtains. But
except for his scythe he
had nothing at all.

"My patterns?" he said.
"Oh, I have them all,
though you can't see
them just at the moment.
Every one makes a pattern of his life, you know. Your brother
does. Your friends do. You do. I'll show you any pattern
you like to ask me for."

"Well—I'd like to see what pattern my brother made last year," said Robin.

Father Time put down his scythe carefully. He put out the light. Then he held up his hands in the darkness and from the fingers of Old Father Time there flowed a shining ribbon, broad and quivering as if it were alive. It was as wide as the table, and it flowed down on to it like a cloth, spreading itself flat for Robin to see.

"I say! It's a lovely pattern," said Robin. "I shouldn't have thought my little brother could have made such a beauty. How did he make it?"

"The pattern is made of the stuff he put into each day," said Father Time. "The happy moments—the times he ran to do a kindness—the times he cried with fear or pain. They are all in the pattern. This line of silver is a line of love—he loves very much—for it is a beautiful line. This glowing thread shows his happy times—he is a happy little boy. This shimmering piece is a great kindness he did, about the middle of the

year. It shines because it still shines in every one's memory."

"Yes—I remember that," said Robin. "I hurt my leg and couldn't go to a party. So Lennie wouldn't go either, and he brought me every single one of his toys and gave me them for my own, because he was so sorry for me—even his best railway train that he loves. I shall never forget how kind he was to me. But what is this ugly little line of black dots that keeps showing in the pattern?"

"Those spots come into a pattern when the maker of the pattern loses his temper," said Father Time. "He must be careful, or as the years go on the spots will get bigger and bigger and spoil his pattern altogether."

"Oh dear—I'll have to warn him," said Robin. "Now show me Harry's pattern, Father Time. You know—Harry Jones. He lives next door. Have you got his for last year?"

"Yes, I collected it tonight," said Father Time. The pattern he had been showing Robin faded away into the darkness, and from Father Time's fingers flowed another one that spread itself on the table as the other had done.

It was an ugly pattern, with two or three bright threads lighting it up. Robin looked at it.

"It's not a very beautiful pattern, is it?" he asked.

"No. Harry cannot have done well with his three hundred and sixty-five days last year," said Father Time sadly. "See— that horrid mess there means greediness and selfishness—and here it is again—and again—spoiling the pattern that the bright threads are trying to make."

"Yes—Harry *is* selfish," said Robin. "He's an only child, and thinks everything must be for him. What are the bright threads, Father Time?"

Father Time looked at them closely. "They are fine strong bits of pattern," he said. "They are the hard work that Harry has done. He is a good worker, and if he goes on trying hard,

those bright threads will be so strong that they will run right through those messy bits. Maybe one day he will make a better pattern."

The pattern faded. Robin thought for a moment, and then he asked for another. "Show me Elsie's, please," he said. "She's such a nice girl. I like her."

Once again a pattern flowed over the table. It was a brilliant one, beautiful and even. It would have been quite perfect except that it seemed to be torn here and there.

"It's lovely except for those torn bits," said Robin.

"Yes—Elsie must be a happy and clever girl," said Father Time. "But alas—look at these places where the pattern is quite spoilt! That means cruelty, Robin—a thing that tears the pattern of our lives to bits. Poor Elsie! She must be careful, or one day her pattern will be torn to pieces, and all her happiness will go."

"How strange, Father Time!" said Robin, astonished. "That's the one thing I can't bear about Elsie—she is so unkind to animals. I've often seen her throw stones at them. And yet she's so nice in every other way."

"Tell her about her pattern," said Father Time. "For maybe one day a moment of cruelty will spoil a whole year or more."

"Now show me Leslie's pattern," said Robin. "He's such a funny little boy, Father Time—so shy and timid, like a mouse! I'd love to see the kind of pattern that he has made this last year."

Once again a pattern flowed in the darkness—but what a queer one! It could hardly be seen. There was no brightness in it, no real pattern to see. It was just a smudge of dingy colours.

"Poor little boy!" said Father Time. "He is afraid of everything! He has put no brightness into his pattern, no happy moments, no kindness—only shyness and fear. Robin, you must help him to make a better pattern next year. Tell him to have courage and not to be afraid of doing kindness to anyone—then his pattern will glow and shine."

The pattern faded. Father Time went to switch on the light. "I must go," he said. "I have many other patterns to collect tonight, and to put into my book of history."

"Wait a minute!" said Robin. "Please, Father Time—may I see my own pattern?"

"Yes, you may," said Father Time. He didn't put on the light but held up his strange fingers once again. And from them flowed the pattern of all the days of the last year—the pattern made by Robin himself.

Robin looked at it, half fearful, half excited, wondering what he would see. He saw a brilliant pattern, full of bright colours that danced and shone. In it were pools of silver light, but here and there were smudges of grey that spoilt the lovely pattern he had made.

"Ah, Robin, you have done well this year to make such a fine pattern," said Father Time, pleased. "You have been happy, for see how the pattern glows. You have worked hard, for see how strong the pattern is, unbroken and steady. You have been kind, for here are the silver pools that shine in the pattern and shine in your friends' memories, too."

"But, Father Time—what are those grey smudges that spoil the pattern here and there?" asked Robin, puzzled. "I don't like them."

"Neither do I," said Father Time. "They show where you spoilt your days by telling untruths, Robin. Truth always shines out in a pattern, but untruths smudge it with grey. See—you did not tell the truth there—and there—and there— and look, as the pattern reaches the end of the year, the grey smudges got worse. You have let that bad habit grow on you and spoil the lovely pattern you were making."

"Yes," said Robin, ashamed. "I have been getting worse

about telling untruths, I know. Mother keeps telling me that. I didn't know that they would spoil the pattern of my year, though. I'll be very, very careful next year—I shan't tell a single untruth, then my pattern will be really lovely."

"Be careful nothing else creeps in to spoil it," said Father Time. "I will come next year and show you the pattern you have made. Now good-bye—I must go. I feel much warmer and I have enjoyed our talk!"

"So have I! It was wonderful," said Robin. "Thank you very much, Father Time!"

The old man slipped out of the house and Robin went back to bed. He dreamed all night long of the year's patterns, and when he awoke in the morning he couldn't think whether it had *all* been a dream or not.

"Anyway, I shall know next New Year's Eve," said Robin. "I shall look out for the old man again then—and see the pattern I have made! I do hope it's beautiful."

Would you like to see the one you made last year? What do you think it would be like? I *would* love to know!

ROSE PETALS

The pixies come each day and take
The petals from the ground,
Silken eiderdowns they make
Neatly stitched all round.
They never mind the wintry days
For then in bed they creep,
Beneath their eiderdowns they laze,
Warm and half-asleep!

THE LAVENDER HEDGE

The lavender hedge has grown so tall
With its fragrant flowers of blue!
And now here I come to spoil it all,
For see what I mean to do!
My scissors flash, and my basket fills
With flowers the colour of distant hills!

But you will not die as others must
Sweet lavender, slim and blue—
You will not fade, and fall in the dust,
You'll blossom the whole year through!
In cupboard and drawer, in box and in chest
You'll breathe out the fragrance I love the best!

YOU CAN'T CATCH ME!

Sea! Sea!
You can't catch me!
I'm dancing about on the beach,
Your waves come out,
And splash about,
But my toes you cannot reach!

Sea! Oh sea!
You are tricking me!
You sent a big wave so far
That it wetted my frock—
I *did* get a shock!
Oh, what a bad fellow you are!

THE WIND

Blow, Wind, blow today!
  Swing the weather-cock round!
Hurry the clouds in the sky away,
  And bend the grass to the ground!
Hurry and scurry and puff and blow,
  Making the tall trees sway,
I'd like to be with you wherever you go,
  Blow, Wind, today!

The Adventure of the Secret Door

"WE shall be dreadfully bored, staying with Great-Aunt Hannah," said Dick, gloomily. "She's nice and kind —but there's absolutely nothing to do at Westroofs."

"What's the house like?" asked Lucy. "You've been there, Dick—Robin and I haven't."

"Well, it's awfully old—and rather dark inside—and there's a big room called the Library, which is lined from floor to ceiling with the dullest books you ever saw—and at night the ivy taps on the window-pane and makes you jump!" said Dick.

"Here we are!" said Robin, peering out of the car window as they swung through a pair of enormous old gates. "My word —it *is* an old house—look at the ivy covering it from roof to ground!"

Great-Aunt Hannah was waiting to welcome them. She was a dear old lady, with snow-white hair, pink cheeks and a very kind smile.

"Welcome to Westroofs!" she said. "I do so hope you won't find it dull, my dears. But when I heard that your mother was ill, I really thought it would be a kindness to her to have you here for a while."

The three children felt sure that they would be very dull indeed at Westroofs. There were no horses to ride, no dogs to take for a walk, and not even a cat with kittens to play with. Still, if only the weather was fine, they could go for walks and explore the country round.

But the weather wasn't fine. When they awoke the next morning, the rain was pouring down, and it went on all day long. The children roamed about the house, not daring to play any exciting games in case they disturbed Aunt Hannah, who jumped at any sudden shout or stamping of feet.

Next day it was still raining, and the children felt quite desperate. "I've never been so bored in my life," groaned Dick. "Whatever can we do? Let's go out in the rain."

But Aunt Hannah was afraid they would get wet and catch cold. "No, don't go out," she said. "Wouldn't you like to go and look at the books in the library? There are some that belonged to my great-grandfather when he lived at Westroofs. Very, very interesting."

The children didn't feel as if Great-Aunt Hannah's great-grandfather's books would be at all interesting, but they were much too polite to say so. They went into the big, dark library, and switched on the middle light, for it was a very dull day.

"There must be hundreds and hundreds of books here nobody ever reads or wants to read," said Dick, looking at the crowded, dusty shelves. "Here's one that I'm sure nobody has ever read—*History of Edward Lucian*, born 1752, in the parish of Elham. Why, half the pages are still uncut. Poor Edward Lucian."

"Lucian is our family name. Perhaps he was a great-great-great-ancestor of ours," said Robin. "Look, here's a ladder in this corner. Whatever is it for?"

"To climb up to the topmost shelves, I should think, if anyone should ever want a book from there," said Lucy. "Let's pull it up. We'll see what kind of books they kept on the top shelf. Do you suppose there are any story-books at all?"

"Shouldn't think so," said Robin, putting the ladder up by the shelves of books. "Well, here I go. If I see anything exciting, I'll toss it down."

Up he went. The top shelf was covered with thick grey dust. It flew into the air as Robin pulled out one or two books, and made him sneeze. The sneeze made him drop a book, and it almost fell on Lucy's head.

"Look out, idiot," said Lucy, as the book crashed to the floor. It fell half-open, and something flew out of the pages.

"There! One of the pages has got loose," said Lucy. "I'll put it back in its right place."

But when she picked it up, she saw that it was not a loose page, but an old, old letter, written on a half-sheet of paper, in curious old-fashioned writing. She could hardly make out a word. She held it out to Dick.

"Look at this old letter," she said. "All the s's are f's. It's impossible to read."

Robin came down the ladder. He too looked at the queer letter. He and Dick began to spell it out slowly.

"Today—I went through—the Secret Door. I have hid my new top there, and the stick I cut from the hedge. William shall not have them. He knows not the way through—through —the Secret Door. He is not —not—allowed in the Sad— Sad—what *is* this word—oh, *Saddle*. He is not allowed in the Saddle Room, and knows not the Secret Panel there."

The writing ended at that point. The three children were suddenly seized with great excitement. They stared at one another feeling rather breathless.

"It's not a letter—it must be part of a diary or something— kept by some—a boy—who lived here years and years ago."

"And he had a brother called William. And William didn't know about a Secret Panel in the Saddle Room, or about a Secret Door. Golly! Let's go and explore! We might find them."

"Where's the Saddle Room? Oh, I know—it's the little room at the side of the house, near where the old stables used to be. And it's got panelling all round the walls, I remember! Quick, let's go!"

Forgetting all about putting the ladder back in its corner, or the book back in its place, the children ran out of the dark library, down long passages, and came to the Saddle Room.

It was a low, dark room, set round with squared oak panels. Even now there were two or three old saddles hanging on nails, and a crop lay on a shelf. The rest of the room contained chairs and tables turned out from other rooms. It was plainly a kind of store-room now.

"Now—which would be the secret panel?" said Dick, looking round the walls. "Golly, isn't this exciting? Where shall we try first? Not on that wall, because it's almost covered by that big old picture. Let's try over here by the fireplace."

"How do we look for a secret panel, and what does it do?" asked Lucy. "Do we press or push or what?"

"A secret panel was usually put into a wall of panelling to conceal a cupboard, or some sort of secret way out or in," said Dick. "We must press each one, and jiggle it, and see if we can make one move."

Dick began to knock round the walls. "Thud, thud, thud."

"I might hear if one panel sounds hollow," he said. "If it did, I'd know it might be the secret one."

But none of them sounded hollow. It was most disappointing. "Perhaps the panel is behind that big picture after all," said Dick. "Let's move it."

But they couldn't. It was much too heavy. They gazed round the little room in despair. Then Dick went to where a saddle hung on a great nail, and took it down. "I haven't tried *this* panel," he said, and knocked on it. It sounded hollow.

"It must be the one!" cried Lucy, and they all pushed at the brown, polished panel, and banged on it. But nothing happened. In desperation Dick caught hold of the big nail and pulled at it.

And then, before their eyes, the panel slid downwards a little, and then sideways, quite soundlessly. Behind it was a dark space. The children stared breathlessly.

"We've found it! We've found the Secret Panel. What's in the hole?"

Dick sped off for his torch, and soon the children were peering into the hole left by the sliding panel. There didn't seem anything to see at all—just a hole, dark and empty.

"Well—if that isn't disappointing!" said Robin. "Just a hole. And anyway, where's this Secret Door we read about? There's no door here. Nobody could get through this hole."

Dick put his hand right into the dark hole and groped round. His hand suddenly found what seemed to be a handle or knob of some kind. He pulled it.

Behind the children came a sudden grating noise, then a terrific crash. They all jumped violently, very frightened. They looked round, scared.

"It's that big picture. It fell off the wall," said Dick. "And my goodness—look—there's a space behind it. It's the Secret Door!"

The children stared in delight. There was an opening in the panelling where the great picture had been, an opening big enough to get through! Where did it lead to?

"When I pulled that knob in the hole here—it must have worked something that opened the Secret Door," said Dick. "And when it opened, the picture had to fall, of course. Golly, it did make me jump!"

A deep sound suddenly boomed through the house. "No good—it's dinner-time!" said Lucy, with a groan. "Just as we have found this exciting Secret Door!"

"Better shut it up again," said Dick. "We won't say a word to Aunt Hannah about it till we've explored a bit. We might find family treasure, or something. You never know!"

Visions of glittering jewels, bars of silver and gold, boxes of coins, flashed into the minds of the children. It was very hard to pull at the knob inside the hole and see the Secret Door shut itself, when they so badly wanted to go through it. They couldn't lift the heavy picture up again, so they left it standing against the wall. Then they went to wash their hands.

Aunt Hannah beamed at them as they took their places at the table. "Well," she said, "it has stopped raining at last—and I have arranged a treat for you this afternoon."

The children looked blank. A treat? The only treat they wanted was to go through that Secret Door! Why had the rain stopped? They didn't want to leave the house now.

"I've telephoned to Farthington—that's our nearest big town, you know," said Aunt Hannah, "and I've got tickets for the circus there, for you. A car is coming at half-past two, and you shall have a late tea at a very nice shop in Farthington that has chocolate éclairs and meringues."

Now ordinarily this would have been a simply glorious treat, but not today. Still, as it was all arranged, the children could do nothing but say thank you, and go!

"We'll have to explore this evening," said Dick, gloomily. "I can hardly wait! What a pity the circus couldn't have been tomorrow."

It was a lovely circus, and the tea that followed was glorious. Aunt Hannah came too and seemed to enjoy everything very much. "Now, when we get home, we will all have a quiet game of cards together," she said. "I don't want you to get over-excited tonight, after such an exciting afternoon."

So once again exploring had to be put off, and the children played Happy Families and Cheating till bed. It was terribly disappointing.

Just as Lucy was about to fall asleep in her bed that night, the two boys came cautiously into her room. "Lucy! Are you awake? We're going to go through that Secret Door now, tonight! We simply can't wait. Do you want to come, or will you be frightened, because it's night?"

"Of *course* I want to come!" said Lucy, wide-awake immediately. "I'll put on my dressing-gown at once. Oh, how super! I never, never thought you'd go tonight!"

Trembling with excitement Lucy followed the two boys downstairs, and along the passages that led to the Saddle Room. Dick pulled at the nail that opened the Secret Panel. It swung aside as before. He put in his hand and pulled at the knob behind. With a grating noise the Secret Door opened in the panelling nearby, and the children stared into the gaping hole.

Dick shone his torch there. "A short passage, then steps," he said, in excitement. "Come on!"

He stepped through the Secret Door, and the others followed. The passage was very short, and ended at some narrow, very steep stone steps that led downwards. Dick felt hot with excitement. Where did they lead to?

He went down cautiously, afraid of falling. The others followed. There were fifteen of these steps, then they ended, and another passage came in sight.

"We must be below ground now!" called Dick. "Here's

another passage—leading away from the house. I do wonder what it used to be for!"

"Oh, most old houses had secret passages or hiding-places," said Robin. "People in olden days often needed to hide their treasure from enemies—or even to hide themselves. Golly, isn't it dark —and the roof's so low just here I have to bend my head."

It was very weird, walking along the narrow, musty passage so far underground. It curved about to avoid rocky parts. Then suddenly Dick came to a standstill.

"Blow! There's been a fall here! Look. The roof has fallen in and we can't get by."

The others crowded up to him and looked over his shoulder. "Yes, we *can* get by," said Robin. "We can kick away the rubble at this side, look—and make a way through. It's easy."

They did manage to make their way through and then, covered with dust, they came to a small, underground room! An old bench stood at one side,

and a crock for water. On a rough shelf was a dust-covered top, and a queer, curved stick. The children gazed at them in delight.

"The top and the stick—that that boy of long ago hid from Brother William," said Dick at last. "How weird. He never came to fetch them again."

They stood in silence, looking round the bare little room—and then Robin gave an amazed cry. He bent down and picked up something. "Look," he said, "do look—*a cigarette* end!"

So it was. The others could hardly believe their eyes. "How did it get here? Who has been here? And when?"

As they stood there they suddenly heard a noise. It seemed to come from above their heads. They looked up and saw that the roof seemed to have a hole in it.

And then, even as they looked, the end of a rope appeared, and the rope itself slid through the hole and touched Dick on the shoulder. He shut off his torch at once.

"Someone's coming! But what do they do here? It's almost midnight. They must be up to something queer!"

"Get back to where that fall of rubble is," whispered Robin. "We can squeeze through again, and stay at the other side and listen. Quick!"

With beating hearts the three hurried to the mass of rubble, squeezed through as quietly as they could, and then stood waiting in the dark, listening and peering through the cracks in the heap of rubble that stretched from floor to roof.

Someone slid down the rope. Then a torch flashed on. "Come on, Bill," said a voice. "Buck up with the stuff!"

The man took a candle from his pocket, and set it on the wooden bench. He lighted it and the children saw by its flickering flame that the man in the underground room was thick-set and very short. As he stood there, waiting, something fell through the hole in the roof, and the man caught it deftly. Then another package came, looking like a sack of something, and then another.

A muffled voice sounded down the hole. "That's all, Shorty. Come on up. We'll fetch it tomorrow."

Shorty hauled himself up the rope, after blowing out the candle. Then there was silence. The children waited for a while, then cautiously made their way back to the underground room again. There were now three sacks there, tied up at the necks.

"They're full of something hard," said Dick, feeling them. "Got a knife on you, Robin?"

Nobody had, because they all wore dressing-gowns. Robin managed to untie one of the sacks. It was full of little jewel boxes. Lucy opened one, and gasped.

Inside was a most beautiful necklace, that glittered brilliantly in the light of the torch. All the other boxes contained jewellery too.

"Looks like the result of a very successful robbery!" said Dick. "What a wonderful place to hide it! I suppose the burglars didn't know there was another way to this room, besides that hole in the roof. What shall we do? Drag the sacks back to the house?"

"Oh *yes*," said Lucy. "They will be such a surprise for Great-Aunt Hannah. I'd love to see her face when she sees all these. And it would be too awful to leave them here, in case these men came back and got them!"

So puffing and panting, the children dragged a sack each through the rubble and up the passage to the stone steps. Up the steps they went and along to the Secret Door. They dumped the sacks in the Saddle Room and sat down, panting and excited.

"You go and wake Aunt Hannah, Lucy," said Dick. So she went up to her Great-Aunt's room and knocked on the door.

"What is it?" came Aunt Hannah's startled voice. "Oh, you, Lucy. Is somebody ill?"

"No. But, Aunt Hannah, do put on your dressing-gown and come down to the Saddle Room," begged Lucy.

"To the *Saddle* Room—in the middle of the night!" said Aunt Hannah, beginning to think it was all a dream. "Dear, dear—whatever's happening!"

Soon she was down in the Saddle Room, astonished to see the big sacks there, and even more astonished to see the Secret Door.

"Good gracious!" she said, "so you've found that! The Door has not been used for ages—and has been forgotten so long that nobody ever knew where it was—except you children, apparently! Well, well, well—now tell me what's been happening."

So they told her—and when they showed her what was in the sacks Great-Aunt Hannah could hardly believe her eyes. She gasped and blinked, and couldn't find a word to say.

"I suppose we'd better ring up the police, hadn't we?" said Dick. "We could hand these back, and tell them about the burglars' plan to go to the underground room tomorrow night —they could catch them beautifully!"

The police were amazed, and very pleased. "Ho—so it was Shorty and Bill, was it?" said the Inspector. "Well, we've been wanting them for a very long time! The stolen goods all belong to the Duchess of Medlington—my word, she'll be glad to have them back! Smart work, children!"

"Well, it was all because of William's brother, really," said Lucy, and the Inspector stared at her in surprise. William's brother? Whatever was the child talking about?

"Now you really must go to bed, children," said Aunt Hannah. "It's two o'clock in the morning. Shocking! No more finding of Secret Doors and Underground Rooms and Stolen Goods tonight, please. Off to bed with you!"

"Well," said Dick, as they got into bed at last, "we thought this would be the dullest place in the world to stay at—but it's given us a Most Exciting Adventure."

So it had—and it was even more exciting when the Inspector telephoned the next night to say that he had got Bill and Shorty all right. "You can't think how astonished they were when they found that their sacks had vanished out of that hole!" chuckled the Inspector. "And they were even more amazed when my men popped down on top of them."

"Wish I'd been there," said Dick. "I say, Aunt Hannah—do you think I might have that long-ago boy's top? It still spins beautifully."

"Of course," said Aunt Hannah. "And Robin can have the walking stick, cut so many, many years ago from the hedge. And as for Lucy, she can have this tiny brooch, which has been sent to her by the Duchess herself! There you are, Lucy—now you will none of you ever forget the adventure of the Secret Room!"

MY GARDEN

Tulips gay and tall,
Bluebells slim and sweet,
Pansies soft and small,
    And daisies round my feet!
Honesty a-glow
    In every shady place,
Poppies on tiptoe,
    Lilac full of grace.
Forget-me-nots so blue,
    Wallflowers all a-shine,
Apple-blossom new—
    I'm glad, I'm glad you're mine!

AUTUMN AND WINTER

AUTUMN has come again, and the summer, with its wealth of flowers and insects, its golden cornfields and its glowing heather commons, has gone.

Let's put on our coats and go for a walk on this lovely autumn day. We shall not see the same things as we saw in the springtime, but we shall see some just as beautiful.

Here we go, down the lane, through the wood and out on the hills. There are not nearly so many flowers to be seen now, but we can still find such common ones as groundsel, ragwort, harebell, thistle, shepherd's purse and so on.

One of the prettiest of the autumn flowers is the meadow saffron, or autumn crocus. We may find it growing in some corner now, looking just like a collection of long-stemmed, pale mauve crocuses. But how queer—they have no leaves! These come up in the springtime, and die down before the flowers bloom.

There is another flower we shall find just coming into bloom. Come down the lane to where the old stump of a tree grows. Covering it is the ivy, holding fast to the old trunk with its finger-like roots. Look at the ivy blossom, its big clusters of greenish-yellow flowers springing from between the dark ivy leaves. The ivy gives the hungry insects their very last feast, for it has plenty of nectar in its blossoms.

Here we can see most of the insects that are still alive and awake in the autumn. Big blue-bottle flies buzz over the flowers, and smaller flies crawl here and there, sucking up the nectar. Bees are there, and a queen wasp in her striped suit. Butterflies feast on the blossoms, too, gay red admirals, tortoise-shells and peacocks, opening and shutting their glowing wings to feel the warm autumn sun.

A great many of the summer insects are dead. Some of them sleep the cold days away. The queen wasp will soon find a cosy corner behind the ivy on a wall, and sleep until the sun awakes her in the springtime. The bees go to their hive to sleep, and the big bumbles find a hole in the ground. They like one that faces north, for they do not want to be waked too soon, for fear they are caught by a frost!

Some of the butterflies on the ivy blossom will hibernate, too. We may find a peacock or a red admiral cuddled up in a corner of our barn or outhouse. Many caterpillars sleep the winter away in chrysalids. No food for them, and no heat—so the sensible thing to do is to go to sleep until the spring comes again!

What a lovely colour the trees are turning now! The chestnut is a splendid golden brown, the hazels are pale yellow, the elms are a glory of gold. The wild cherry turns crimson, and matches the creeper on the cottages nearby. The oak is a russet brown, and the birch a most delicate yellow. Most beautiful of all are the beech woods, for every leaf is now the colour of golden sovereigns, a rich and glorious hue.

Why do the trees change colour in the autumn? They have a very good reason indeed. Soon their leaves will fall, for they do not need them in the winter. So into their leaves the trees send all the waste matter they do not want—and it is this that changes the leaves to such wonderful colours! We will pick some of them and hold them up to the sun to admire their glowing reds and oranges and yellows.

Soon the leaves will fall, and the trees will be bare. Even now we can see the many-coloured leaves flutter here and there in the wind, and come to the ground. The oak will hold its foliage the longest.

Look at that squirrel! He is bounding up and down the trees. Now he has found something—is it an acorn he is nibbling? What is he doing now? He has come down to the ground and he is busy burying something under a heap of leaves. We will go and see what he has hidden.

Under the leaves is a small pile of hazel nuts. The squirrel, knowing that he will sometimes awake on a warm day in the winter, is preparing a few little hoards of food for himself.

Then, when he awakes hungry, he will go to his hiding-place and find his nuts—that is, if he can remember where he put them! And even if he does remember it is likely that that small mouse we see, peeping out from its hole, will have found them first and taken them away.

There are not only nuts to be found now, but blackberries, too. Other trees bear their fruit as well—the oak has its smooth acorns, set in their pretty cups. The ash is sending its "keys" spinning to the ground, a very fine way of sending off its seeds. The maple and the sycamore are doing the same, and have given little wings to their seeds to help them to find a new home.

The chestnut tree flings its prickly cases to the ground, where they burst and let out the satin-smooth brown "conkers" we like so much. The beech tree throws its seed cases down, too, and the squirrel nibbles at the curious nuts inside. There are cones on the pine trees, and it is fun to gather up the dry fallen ones to take home for the fire.

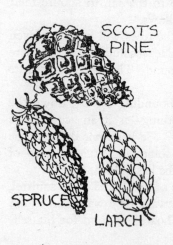

SCOTS PINE

SPRUCE

LARCH

The hawthorns are full of crimson haws. How the birds will love these in the cold winter days! They have picked the mountain ash berries already and are stripping the elder trees of their purple fruit. But not many birds or animals eat the little purple plums in the hedge—the sloes. Why not? Well, we'll taste one and see. Oh, how sour, and how dry it makes our tongue!

Shall we collect some berries? There are some lovely scarlet hips on the wild rose bushes. We will put some haws with them. The honeysuckle has bright red berries, too, but they are very poisonous—as poisonous as the curious waxen-looking berries of the dark yew trees.

What are these berries, hanging on a long spray in the hedge? They are bryony, and we will take some. If we can find some spindle-tree berries, we really must have those, too, for they are beautiful. The outer part of the berry is brilliant orange and the seed inside is a bright pink—how lovely they will be in a vase!

What is this floating lightly through the air? Thistledown! It is the seed of the thistle, given hundreds of tiny silk hairs to fly away on. Ah! look—there are the seeding thistles over there—and on them, twittering sweetly, is a flock of pretty, fairy-like goldfinches, who love the seeds of the thistle.

The woods are damp underfoot now. Fungi grow every-where—saddle-like fungus on the trunks of trees—toadstools, all sizes and colours, on the ground. If we know where to look for them, we may find mushrooms.

On the hills we shall see the curious "fairy rings"—dark circles of grass, where, so the country folk say, the fairies danced last night. What makes them? Well, where the grass is dark, there stood, a few days ago, a ring of champignon toad-stools, the "fairy-ring" toadstools. When they died, they enriched the grass, which grew a deeper green. We shall see the circles of toadstools, and also the grassy rings they have left, if we look for them on the hills and fields.

Where are the cuckoos and the swifts? They have gone away. The swallows and martins are still left, because the weather is warm and calm—but do you see that barn roof over there, and the telegraph wires beyond? They are covered with eager, twittering birds, waiting for the signal to dart up and fly away south.

The robin follows us on our walk, ticking away in the hedge. He often makes this curious clicking noise now, but sometimes he bursts into song and other robins answer him. In these autumn days each robin marks out his own domain, his "beat," and he will not allow any other robin to come into it. "No!" he sings, "there is only enough food for one here! Go away! This garden is mine." If the other robin dares to come any further, he will fight him furiously.

Where are the frogs? It is no good looking for them on our walk. They are down in the muddy pond, asleep. The bats are preparing to hibernate, too, and if we peep into that old barn we may find some already asleep for the winter, hanging upside down, covered with their queer "hand wings".

The snakes are sleeping now, curled up in a knot in a hollow tree. Under that stone we may find a sleeping toad, for the nights have been cold, and he may already be asleep. Yes, here he is—and with him are two snails. We will pick them up and look at them. Do you see how they have grown a horny door across the entrance to their shell? They can sleep in safety with that "door" to prevent enemies from creeping inside their house!

Now we must turn homewards again. We will walk through the russet bracken, lovely in its autumn colouring. How tall it has grown since the springtime! Over the springy heather, faded now, but still covered with its dead flowers, and down into the little lane.

What is this lying like grey fluff all over the hedgerow? Have sheep been by and left their grey wool here? No—if we pull at it, we find that the fluffy sprays are growing from a thin, strong stalk. It is old man's beard, the fluffy seeds of the wild clematis. It really does look like an old man's beard and the name has stuck.

Dusk is coming now. Rabbits are out in the fields, and a hare flashes by up the hill. Then something scares the rabbits, and they scurry to their burrows, their white bobtails gleaming a warning as they go. Perhaps it is the red fox.

Not all creatures sleep the winter away. Rabbits and hares, weasels, stoats and foxes are all awake. We shall see them in our autumn walks and in our winter ones as well. The rats and mice are awake, too—but the little dormouse, or dozy mouse, makes himself fat, and then goes to sleep so soundly that it is difficult to awake him if we find him.

HARE

The starlings come along in a big flock, and play together for a while in the sky whilst we stand and watch them. Then down they drop all together into the bushes where they roost. Chaffinches fly by in a flock, too, having been busy seeking for seeds in the farmyard. Many birds flock together when the cold days come, and hunt for food, liking each other's company.

Now what is that—a great cloud of small birds flying through the evening sky. We heard their familiar twitter, *feetafeetit, feetafeetit,* and we know they are swallows. They are leaving us. They will leave England tonight and will make a leisurely journey across Europe and down into Africa, a land of warmth and plenty.

But when the spring comes they will turn homewards again —for this is their home, where they build their nests and bring up their young.

And now, here we are, back again, after a lovely walk. We bring pine cones for the fire, berries for the vases, and acorns and chestnuts to plant in little pots to grow as trees. A walk in the country—not many things nicer than that!

The Enchanted Egg

Now once upon a time Sly-One the gnome did a marvellous piece of magic that nobody had ever done before.

He stirred together in a golden bowl, lit by moonlight, many peculiar things. One of them was the breath of a bat, another was a snippet of lightning, and yet another was an echo he had got from a deep cave.

He didn't quite know what would come of all these strange things and the dozens of others he had mixed together—but he guessed it would be something very powerful indeed.

"Whatever it is, it will bring me greatness and power," thought Sly-One, stirring hard. "I shall be able to do what I like."

Sly-One was not a nice person. He was mean and unkind and sly. Nobody liked him, though most people were afraid of him because he was very cunning. But he did not use his brains for good things, only for bad ones.

He stirred away for two whole hours, and soon the curious mixture in the golden bowl began to turn a colour that Sly-One had never in his life seen before. Then it began to boil! As it boiled, it twittered!

"Very strange indeed," said Sly-One to himself, half scared. "A very curious twitter indeed. It sounds like the twitter of the Magic Hoolloopolony Bird, who hasn't been seen for five hundred years. Surely this magic mixture of mine isn't going to make a Hoolloopolony Bird! How I wish it was, because if I had that bird I could do anything I liked. It is so magic that it has the power to obey every order I give it. Why, I could be king of the whole world in a day!"

But the mixture didn't make a bird. It twittered for a little while longer, turned another curious colour, and then boiled away to nothing.

Or almost nothing. When Sly-One, disappointed, looked into the bowl, he saw something small lying at the bottom of it. It was a tiny yellow egg, with a red spot at each end.

Sly-One got very excited indeed when he saw it. "It's not a Hoolloopolony Bird—but it's the egg! My word, it's a Hoolloopolony Egg! Now, if only I can get it hatched, I shall have one of those Enchanted Birds for my very own—a slave that can obey any order I think of making!"

He picked up the egg very gently. It hummed in his fingers and he put it back into the bowl. How was he to get it hatched?

"I'd better find a bird's nest and put it there," thought Sly-One. "A really fine nest, safe and warm and cosy, where this enchanted egg can rest and be hatched out. I must go round and inspect all the nests there are. I shall soon find a good one."

He left the egg in the bowl, and covered it with a silver sheet. Then he put on his hat and went out. It's the nesting season for birds, and Sly-One knew there would be plenty of nests to choose from.

He soon found one. It was a robin's, built in a ditch. Sly-One walked up to inspect it, and knelt down beside it.

"It's made of moss and dead leaves and bits of grass," he said. "It's well-hidden because there are plenty of dead leaves lying all round. Perhaps this will do."

But just then a dog came sniffing into the ditch and Sly-One changed his mind. "No, no! It's not a good place for a nest, if dogs can tramp about near it. Why, that dog might easily put his paw on the Enchanted Egg and smash it, if I put it here!"

So he went off to find another nest. He saw some big ones

high up in a tree and he went to look at them. They were rooks' nests, big and roomy.

"They look safe enough, high up there," thought Sly-One. "Made of good strong twigs too. No dog could tread on *these* high nests!"

He sat down in one to see what it was like. Just then a big wind blew and the tree rocked the nest violently. Sly-One was frightened. He climbed out quickly.

"Good gracious!" he said to the rooks, "I wonder you build your nests quite so high in the trees! The wind will blow your nests to and fro and out will come your eggs!"

"Caw!" said a big rook, scornfully. "Don't you know that when a stormy summer is expected we build lower down and when a calm one comes, we build high up? We always know! No wind will blow our nests down. Why do you come to visit them, Sly-One? You don't lay eggs!"

Sly-One didn't answer. He slid down the tree, and came to a hole in the trunk. He put his head in and saw a heap of sawdust

at the bottom. It was a little owl's nest. Sly-One felt about, and didn't like it.

"Not at all comfortable for an Enchanted Egg," he thought. "A good idea though for a nest, deep down in a tree-hole. Very very safe!"

"If you want another kind of hole, ask the kingfisher to show you his," hissed the little owl. "Do you want to hide from your enemies or something, Sly-One? Then the kingfisher's nest is just the place!"

So Sly-One went to the brilliant kingfisher, who sat on a low branch over the river and watched for fish. "Where is your nest?" asked Sly-One.

"Down there, in that hole in the bank," said the kingfisher, pointing with his big strong beak. "Right at the end. You'll see it easily."

Sly-One found the hole and crawled into it. At the end was a queer nest, made of old fish-bones arranged together. It smelt horrible.

"I feel sick!" said Sly-One, and crawled out quickly. "Fancy making a nest of smelly old fish-bones! Certainly I shan't put my precious Enchanted Egg there!"

He saw the house-martins flying in the air above him and he called to them. "Where are your nests? I want to find a nice, cosy, safe one to put something precious in."

"See that house?" said a house-martin, flying close to him. "See the eaves there? Well, just underneath we have built our nests. They are made of mud, Sly-One."

"What!" said Sly-One, looking up at the curious mud-nests in amazement. "Are those your nests—those queer things made of mud, stuck against the walls of the house? They might

fall down at any minute! And fancy living in a *mud*-nest! No, that won't do, thank you."

"Coo-ooo," said a wood-pigeon, flying near. "Would *my* nest do for you, Sly-One? I don't know what you want it for —but I have a very nice nest indeed."

"What's it made of?" asked Sly-One.

"Oh—just two sticks across and a little bit of moss!" said the wood-pigeon, and showed Sly-One the tree in which she had built her nest.

"Why, you can see right through it, it's so flimsy!" said Sly-One, in horror, thinking that his Enchanted Egg would certainly fall through the pigeon's nest, and land on the ground below.

Then he went to the lark, but the lark said that she just laid her eggs in a dent in the ground. She showed him her eggs, laid in a horse's hoof-mark in a field.

"Ridiculous!" said Sly-One. "Why, anyone might run over those eggs and smash them. A most stupid place for a nest. I want somewhere that nobody could possibly tread in."

"Well," said the lark, half-offended, "why not go up to the steep cliffs, then, where some of the sea-birds lay their eggs. Look, do you see the great bird there? He's a guillemot. Call him down and ask him to carry you to where he puts his eggs. They are up on the steep cliffs, where nobody can even climb."

Soon Sly-One was being carried on the guillemot's strong wing to the high cliff. There, on a ledge, was a big egg, laid by the guillemot.

"Do you mean to say you just put it there on this ledge?" said Sly-One. "It might fall off at any moment, when the wind blows strongly."

"Oh no it won't," said the guillemot. "Do you see its queer shape? It's made that way, narrow at one end, so that when the

wind blows, it just rolls round and round in the same place. It doesn't fall off."

"Oh," said Sly-One. He thought of his Enchanted Egg. No, that wasn't the right shape to roll round and round. It would certainly roll right off the cliff, if the wind blew. It wouldn't be any good putting it there and asking the guillemot to hatch it for him.

He went to see a few nests made of seaweed, that other sea-birds showed him. But they smelt too strong, and he didn't like them. He went back to the wood near his home, wondering and wondering what nest would be best for his precious egg.

He saw a long-tailed tit go to her nest in a bush. He parted the branches and looked at it. It was a most extraordinary ball-shaped little nest, made of hundreds and hundreds of soft feathers! Perhaps it would be just right for the Hoolloopolony Egg.

"There's no room for another egg," said the long-tailed tit. "I have to bend my long tail right over my head as it is, when I sit in my ball of a nest. When my eleven eggs hatch out, there won't be any room at all!"

Then Sly-One met a big grey bird, with a barred chest. The bird called "Cuckoo!" to him and made him jump.

"Oh, cuckoo, so you're back again," said Sly-One. "Where's your nest?"

"I don't make one," said the cuckoo. "I always choose a good cosy, safe nest to put my eggs in, belonging to somebody else. I don't bother about building!"

"Well," said Sly-One, "as you're used to finding good nests for your eggs, perhaps you can help me. I want one for an Enchanted Egg. I want a good safe nest, with a bird who will hatch out my egg and look after the baby bird for me, till it's old enough to come to me and do magic spells."

"Ah, I'm the one to help you then," said the cuckoo at once. "I can pick up eggs in my beak easily. I've just put an egg into a wagtail's nest. Wagtails make good parents. I'll put your Hoolloopolony Egg there too, if you like."

And that's just what the cuckoo did. She fetched the little egg from the golden bowl, took it in her beak, and popped it into the wagtail's nest up in the ivy. She showed Sly-One her own egg there too.

"The wagtail had four eggs of her own," she said. "I took one out and dropped it on the ground when I put my own there. I've taken a second one out now to make room for your Enchanted Egg. The wagtail will sit on all four eggs and keep them warm, mine, yours, and two of her own."

Sly-One was pleased. "Now my egg will be safe," he thought. "How clever the cuckoo is! She's used to finding good nests for her eggs. I ought to have asked her advice at first, instead of wasting my time inspecting all those other nests."

One day Sly-One went to see how his egg was getting on, and to his surprise the cuckoo's egg had already hatched, though it had been laid after the wagtail's eggs. And also to his surprise, there was only one wagtail egg in the nest, besides his own Enchanted Egg. Sly-One saw the other one lying broken on the ground. He wondered what had happened.

He didn't know the habits of the baby cuckoo. That little

bare, black baby-bird didn't like anything in the nest with him. He had actually pitched the wagtail's egg out of the nest! Now he was lying resting, waiting for strength to pitch the other eggs out too!

He did pitch out one egg—the other wagtail egg. He waited till the mother wagtail was off the nest for a few minutes, then he set to work. He got the wagtail egg into a little hollow on his back, climbed slowly up the side of the nest—and then over went the little egg to the ground below. Another egg gone. Now there was only the Hoolloopolony Egg left to deal with. The baby cuckoo sank back, exhausted.

Then the Enchanted Egg hatched out into a dainty little

yellow bird, with a red head. It lay in the nest close to the baby cuckoo. When the wagtail came back she looked at the two baby birds and loved them. She didn't know they were not really her own.

"I'll go and fetch grubs for you," she said, and flew off.

As soon as she was gone the baby cuckoo wanted to have the nest all to himself. What was this warm bundle pressing close against him? He didn't like it. In fact he couldn't bear it!

Somehow he managed to get the tiny bird on to his back. Somehow he managed to climb up the side of the nest to the top. He gave a heave—and over the top of the nest went the Hoolloopolony baby, right to the ground below.

It twittered there helplessly. The wagtail came back but didn't notice it. She fed the hungry baby cuckoo and thought what a wonderful child he was. She didn't seem to miss the other at all.

When Sly-One came along to see how his wonderful egg was getting on, he found only the baby cuckoo there in the nest! On the ground lay the tiny Hoolloopolony Bird, almost dead.

Sly-One gave a cry. He picked up the tiny bird and put it

into his pocket to keep it warm. He sped to the Wise Woman with it, and begged her to keep it alive.

"Sly-One," said the Wise Woman, "I know why you want this bird. When it grows, it will be able to do powerful magic for you. Well, Sly-One, you are not a nice person and I am not going to rear up a bird to work for you. It must die!"

Sly-One was very angry. "How was I to know the bad ways of baby cuckoos?" he cried. "The cuckoo is not a good bird. It puts its eggs into other birds' nests and throws out their own eggs. And the baby cuckoo throws them out too, and even throws out the baby birds. They are both bad—but how was I to know?"

"You are not really very clever, Sly-One," said the Wise Woman, softly. "I could have told you the ways of all birds and animals, though you should know them yourself. I am glad you chose the cuckoo to help you! Now you will never own a Hoolloopolony Bird, and you will never be king of the world!"

He wasn't, of course, and a very good thing too. As for the tiny bird, it did live, though Sly-One didn't know. The Wise Woman kept it alive, and then set it free. It is full of magic, but no one knows that. It's no good trying to catch it if you see it, because it can't be caught.

Whose nest would *you* have put the egg into? There are such a lot of different ones to choose from, aren't there?

Moving Day

JACK, Jane and Benjy were excited. They were going to a new house!

"This old one is so dark, and there are other houses all round it," said Jack. "We are going into the country now, Benjy, where we shall see more trees than houses, and plenty of grass everywhere, and wild flowers to pick, and cows in the fields."

"I don't like cows," said Benjy.

"You've never even *seen* a cow except in a picture!" said Jane. "So you don't know."

"I do know," said Benjy. "I don't like animals with horns. I shan't go into the fields if there are cows."

"You're a baby," said Jack. "You're only five, and you're still a baby. I'm nine and Jane's seven. We're big, but you're only a baby."

Benjy screwed up his face, and opened his mouth. He meant to howl as loudly as he could.

"Don't cry," said Jane, quickly. "Mummy said we weren't to quarrel, we were to be good. Soon the big van is coming to take all our things to the new house. You'll see it if you don't cry."

Benjy thought he wouldn't cry. He shut his mouth again, opened his eyes, and ran to the window. He gave a shout.

"The big van's here! Look! Oh, what a most enormous one! And here comes another one too!"

The big vans drew up to the house. Mummy opened the door, and the men let down the back of the first van.

"Now we shall see all our things being put into the van,"

said Jane. "There goes the big table. And there goes Mummy's sewing machine. And there goes Daddy's armchair."

"Will they remember to take our toys?" said Benjy, suddenly. "I must have Monkey, I really must. I can't go to bed without Monkey."

"Well, put him under your arm now and then you'll be certain to have him, because Monkey will be with you," said Jane.

Benjy picked up old Monkey. He was such an old and dirty toy. He had first belonged to Jack, then to Jane and now to Benjy. So they all loved him and thought he was beautiful.

Monkey looked out of the window too. He had a long and dirty tail, a funny face, and loose paws that wagged about. All the grown-ups thought he was dreadful, but the children loved him and always took him away with them wherever they went.

"I shall carry Angela with me," said Jane, "then *she* will be safe too. She's my very best doll."

"And I'll take my aeroplane," said Jack. "I couldn't bear that to be left behind."

Mummy came into the nursery and smiled at them. "You must get yourselves ready now," she said. "Daddy is going to drive us in his car. We shall picnic on the way to our new house, and arrive there, we hope, at just about the same time as the vans do."

So they all packed into the car. There were the three children, Daddy, Mummy, and Hannah, their maid. It was a dreadful squash, and Monkey got sat on, but he didn't mind. Benjy sat on Hannah's knee, and Hannah sat on Monkey, though she didn't know it at first.

Off they went. All the children were excited. How lovely to go to a new house!

"What's our new house called?" asked Jane.

"I don't know," said Mummy. "I think it hasn't a name, only a number. But we will give it a name."

"Wait till we get there and see what it is like, then we'll name it," said Daddy.

They had a picnic by the roadside, and then on they went again—and at last they came to the little village where they were going to live.

It looked nice. There was a green in the middle of it. There was a pond by the green with white ducks swimming on it. "I shall feed them every day," said Benjy, pleased.

There were green fields everywhere, and hedges and trees. It was spring-time, so there were yellow primroses on the banks, and soon the bluebells would be out.

"I like this place," said Jane. "Look, is that a farm, Mummy?"

"Yes. We shall get our butter and our eggs and milk from there," said Mummy. "Look at the cows, Benjy! I do like those red and white ones."

"I don't," said Benjy. "They've got horns."

"Silly boy!" said Mummy. "Cows would look funny without horns. Look, there are sheep too. Soon they will have their thick woolly coats sheared off, and they will look queer and bare."

Big cart-horses went by with a clip-clop noise. They had shaggy hoofs and long whisking tails. The children liked them very much.

"I'm glad we've come to live here," said Jane. "Oh look— is that our house, Mummy? Oh, do say it's our house! It's the nicest one I ever saw!"

A Dear Little House

IT *was* their new house! It was such a pretty one. It was white, with a roof made of thatch. It was long and low, and it had tall red chimneys. The front door was painted blue, and there was a lovely knocker on it.

"The knocker is a man's head!" cried Benjy. "It's a nice smiley head. I'll knock with it."

Knock-knock! The knocker made a very loud noise.

"It *is* a nice home, isn't it, Mummy?" said Jane, as she and Mummy pushed open the little blue gate and walked up the primrose-lined path to the blue front door. "Fancy, we're going to live here!"

The children rushed into the empty house, running all over it, up the stairs and down. "Hannah, look at the cosy kitchen!" cried Jane. "Look, it's got a wide window-ledge for you to put your geranium plants on!"

Hannah was great at growing geraniums. She had twelve plants, some red, some pink and one white. She always had them in the kitchen, and was pleased to see such a nice window-ledge she could put them on, in their new home.

"Where's my room?" cried Benjy. "I want to show Monkey where we are to sleep."

"Your room is a little one tucked up in the roof," said Mummy. "You and Jack are to share it. Go and find it."

Jane had a dear little bedroom too. It looked straight out on to two big cherry trees. She looked at them in delight.

"Mummy! I've got cherry trees outside my window, almost touching it. Oh, Mummy, won't it be lovely when they are out! I shall wake up in the morning and think there is snow outside, but it will be cherry blossom, smelling sweet."

"And in June you will be able to lean out of your window and pick ripe red cherries!" said Jack. "I wish *I* was having this room. Mummy, can't I have a room with cherry trees outside?"

"You've got an apple tree just below your window, if you look," said Mummy. "You will be able to pick apples!"

"This is a most lovely house," said Benjy, happily. "I like it. I like the garden. Come and see it, Jane and Jack."

The garden certainly was lovely. There were a lot of fruit trees in it, plenty of flowers, a big patch of grass, and at the bottom a little stream!

"Oh!" squealed Jane, "a stream, Mummy! Is this stream ours? Do say it is!"

"Well, I suppose the little bit that runs through our garden *is* ours!" said Mummy, smiling. "You will be able to sail your boats there."

"I wish we could keep a duck," said Jane. "Isn't it lovely to have our own stream, Jack? Aren't we going to have fun?"

"Here are the vans at last!" called Hannah from the kitchen door. "Now we can really set to work."

The children rushed to see the vans. The men let down the backs, and began carrying the furniture into the house.

Mummy stood in the hall telling the men where to put it. The children got in the way.

"Now, you go into the garden and play there by yourselves for a bit," said Mummy. "You will be a nuisance here. Go along."

The children went back again into the garden. A wall ran between their garden and the gardens next door. They wondered who lived there.

"We shall get to know lots more people," said Jane. "I

hope they will be nice people, not cross ones, like old Mr. Topple who lived next door to our old house. He once shouted at me because I bumped into him round a corner."

Benjy and Jack felt sure that only nice people could live in such a nice village. They all felt very happy. The wind tossed Jane's curls about, and she held her face up to the breeze.

"Even the wind seems nicer here," she said. "Sort of friendly and playful."

After a while Hannah called to the children. "I've got your tea ready for you. Come along. You must be hungry."

They were very hungry. They raced in and to their delight saw that Hannah had laid their tea on the kitchen table, instead of in the dining-room.

"Oh, Hannah! Are we going to have tea in your nice cosy little kitchen?" said Benjy. "Oh, Hannah, isn't it nice with the old table in it, and your four chairs, and your big rocking-

chair, and the stool—and oh, you've got all your geraniums on the window-ledge already!"

"Yes, and they're going to like being there," said Hannah. "The sun shines in there all day long. My, Benjy, look at your hands! Go and wash them at once. You don't suppose I'm going to have a dirty boy like that sitting down at my nice clean table, do you?"

They all went to wash, and then they sat down to tea. There were new brown bread and butter, jammy buns, and some chocolate cake, so it was a very good tea.

"And milk left by the farm-boy!" said Hannah, pouring out three mugs of creamy milk. "Look at that!"

"Are the other rooms ready yet?" asked Benjy, getting all jammy. "Can we go and see them? Oh—where's Monkey? Where did I put him?"

"He can stay where he is till you've finished tea," said Hannah, firmly. "Any one would think you didn't like that old monkey at all the way you leave him about, Benjy."

"You left him looking at the stream," said Jack. "He's probably fallen in by now."

Benjy looked upset. "Now, don't you tease him," said Hannah. "You get on with your tea, and by the time you've finished, the vans will be gone, and you can go and have a look at the house, and see all the rooms full instead of empty."

The vans had gone by the time tea was over. Mummy put her head in at the door. "We've finished! The house is almost straight—just the curtains to put up and the pictures, and the books to arrange. Come and see."

The children rushed to look round. Benjy gave a squeal when he saw his bedroom and Jack's. It looked lovely, "I

like the way the ceiling suddenly slants down each side," he said. "Doesn't my bed look nice in the corner there? Are my toys in that cupboard, Mummy?"

"No, that's for your clothes," said Mummy. "Your toys are downstairs in the playroom. Did you know you were going to have a proper playroom of your own here?"

The playroom was lovely too. It was a small square room with a glass door that opened on to the garden. All round one side was a cupboard for toys, and all round the other side were shelves for books.

"You can arrange your toys and your books yourselves," said Mummy. "I've had them all put in the middle of the floor for you to sort out by yourselves. And as this is to be your own room, *you* will have to see it is kept tidy and nice."

"Oh, *yes*," said Jane, proudly. "Of course we will, Mummy."

"What are we going to call our nice new house?" said Daddy, coming in. "Any one got a good idea?"

"Cherry Trees," said Jane at once.

"Good idea, but there's another house in the lane with that name," said Daddy.

"We *must* think of a good name," said Benjy, frowning hard. "We simply must. It's such a nice *happy* house."

They all stared at the little boy, and then Mummy laughed.

"Benjy's right." she said. "It *is* a happy house and we hope it always will be. Let's call it Happy-House."

So they did, and very soon the name was painted on the blue gate in big, bold letters. "HAPPY-HOUSE." What a nice name for a dear little house!

Someone Else for Happy-House

VERY soon the family was well settled in at Happy-House. They loved it.

Jane loved her small bedroom that looked out on to the cherry trees. She watched the buds burst into snowy blossom, and lay in bed at night sniffing the sweet scent.

The two boys loved their room too, and Benjy said he was going to count every apple on the tree below the window. The straw thatch of the roof came right over Benjy's window, and the little boy watched a wren making a nest there.

The wren didn't mind Benjy. It didn't even mind Monkey either, when Benjy sat him up at the window to watch. It went on making a hole in the thatch, ready for its little wife to lay eggs in.

The playroom was fun. The children soon arranged all their toys there. The cupboard had three shelves in it, so Jack had the top one, Jane had the middle one, and Benjy had the lowest one. There were three bookshelves too, but only enough books to fill two of them.

"We'll have some vases of flowers on the top shelf," said Jane. "They will look lovely against the pale wall."

"And we can put our Noah's Ark animals round the shelf too," said Benjy. "They don't like being shut up in the ark. They told me so."

So the Noah's Ark animals were put on the shelf too, all in pairs. They looked grand. Mummy said it would be a nuisance to dust the shelf, if she had to move so many animals each day, but Jane said if Mummy would give her a duster, she would do it herself.

So, every day, Jane took the animals off the shelf, dusted it well, and put them back again. Sometimes Benjy put them back for her.

Jane picked flowers for the bowls and jars there too, and loved seeing them against the creamy walls of the playroom. There was a bright blue rug on the floor, and blue curtains at the window, so it really was a very nice playroom.

There was a dolls' house in one corner, and Jack's fort in another. There was a bear on wheels that belonged to Benjy. He growled when you pulled a ring in his back. Benjy was still small enough to ride him.

"I wish we had some geraniums, like Hannah's, to put on *our* window-ledge," said Jane. "They would look so nice."

"I know what *I* wish," said Jack, suddenly. "I wish we could have a puppy!"

"You know we can't," said Jane. "We've asked Mummy heaps and heaps of times, and she's said no."

"Yes, but she only said no because we used to live in a big town, and Mummy doesn't like dogs in a town," said Jack. "She might like dogs in the country. I'll ask her."

So he did. "Mummy, could we have a puppy?" he said. "We do so want one. Could we have one for our very own? We'll look after him so carefully."

"Well—I don't see why you shouldn't, now we've left the town," said Mummy. "But he must be *your* dog, children, and *you* must look after him! You will have to give him his food, wash his dishes, see that he has fresh water, and teach him his manners."

"Oh, Mummy! Of course we will!" cried Jane and flung herself on her mother in delight. "Oh, a puppy of our own! What shall we call him?"

"Wait till we get him before you think of any names," said Mummy.

But they couldn't wait for that.

"I shall call him Scamp," said Benjy.

"No. That's an ordinary name," said Jack. "What about Trusty, or something like that? Or Shadow. That's a good name for a dog. Most dogs follow their master as closely as a shadow."

"No," said Jane, "I shall call him Patter. Dogs' paws always make a pattering noise when they run."

"That's a nice name," said Benjy. "I like that. We'll call him Patter. Pat for short, if we like."

"And Pitter-Patter for long," said Jack, with a laugh. "Oh, dear—I wish we could have him soon."

They hadn't very long to wait. One day they went to the farm to get the butter, and there they saw the little girl belonging to the farmer. She was seven, Jane's age, and she carried a very heavy armful of something.

"Whatever has she got?" said Jack. He soon knew, and gave a yell. "Why, she's got a whole lot of puppies in her arms. Amanda, Amanda! Are those your puppies?"

Amanda stopped and smiled at them over the top of the four wriggling puppies. "Yes, they're all mine," she said.

"Aren't you lucky?" said Benjy. "We want just one puppy, and you've got four!"

"Well," said Amanda, "I'll give you one if you like. They are English sheep-dog puppies—that's their mother over there!"

The children looked and saw Judy, the mother. She had a thick coat of grey hair, and masses of hair fell over her eyes, so that it looked as if she could hardly see.

"Oh. She's nice," said Jane. "Will the puppies be like her? Will their hair fall over their eyes like that?"

"Of course," said Amanda. "Well, which one do you want? They're all fat and cuddly and nice."

One wriggled out of her arms and ran to Benjy. It sat firmly down on the little boy's foot. Benjy was simply delighted.

"This is the one," he said. "This is ours. It came to me at once."

The puppy ran to Jane, making a pattering noise with its tiny feet.

"Patter!" cried Jane, and picked him up. "Pitter-Patter! Would you like to be our puppy?"

He licked Jane's nose and then licked Jack's cheek, as the boy bent over him.

"Pat!" said Jack in delight. "Oh, I do like you. Let me hold him, Jane. Oh, do let me have a turn at him."

So they each had a turn at holding the puppy, whilst Amanda stood with the other three.

"Amanda, I hope you don't mind us taking the very nicest of your puppies," said Jane, feeling rather guilty about it.

"Oh, *he* isn't the nicest," said Amanda, and held another one up. "This is the sweetest."

The others didn't think so. They thought their puppy was the very, very best. "Can we take him home now?" said Jack. "Had we better ask your mother first?"

"I'll ask her," said Amanda, and called out to her mother loudly. "Mummy! Can the children from the Happy-House take one of the pups?"

"Yes, if their mother says so," called back Mrs. Busy.

"I'm *sure* Mummy will think this is exactly our puppy!" said Jane, joyfully. "Come on. We'll take him home and let Mummy see him."

So they ran home, Jane carrying the puppy carefully. He cuddled into her and seemed very happy.

Mummy was in the garden, weeding. Jane rushed at her,

and held the puppy against her mother's cheek. The little thing at once licked her with its pink tongue.

"Oh!" said Mummy, surprised. "Jane, where did you get him? What a darling!"

"From the farm. He's ours, if you say so," said Jane. "Mummy, say so!"

"Of course you can have him," said Mummy. "What shall we call him?"

"Patter," said all three children at once. The puppy gave a tiny yelp. "There, he knows his name already!" said Jane. "Let's go and show him to Hannah."

And so it was that Patter came to Happy-House, and pattered all over the house, even upstairs when he grew big enough. Everybody loved him and he loved everybody. But secretly Benjy was sure that Patter loved *him* most!

Oh, Where can Patter be?

ONE day the children took Patter for a walk. They often took him for walks, and he loved them. He could follow very well at their heels, and he always came when he was called.

"Don't go over the marshy fields," called Mummy, as they set off. "Keep on the dry ones. You haven't your rubber boots on."

Patter jumped around them as they went down the lane. Whenever any one of them said, "Heel, Patter!" he ran behind, and kept his nose so close to Benjy's heel, or to Jane's or Jack's that he bumped against them.

"He's really a very, very good dog," said Jane. "Oh, I say—look at those simply enormous buttercups over there! Let's go and pick a bunch."

They set off towards the big golden buttercups. But they hadn't gone very far before they found that the ground was very wet.

"It's marshy ground," said Jane. "Better go back. You know what Mummy said."

"It's not far to the buttercups," said Jack. "Look—let's jump from tuft to tuft of grass, and then we shall be all right."

So they began to jump—but suddenly Jane slipped and fell right down in the wet field. The water squelched up, and Jane felt her frock being soaked through at the back. Her shoes and stockings were wet too. Jack pulled her up.

"Oh, dear!" said Jane. "Oh, dear, whatever will Mummy say? She said we weren't to go over the marshy fields."

"Let's go back," said Benjy, and he tried to step to the next tuft. But his feet too went into the watery grass, and his shoes were soaked.

It took them quite a long time to get back to dry ground. Jack was the only one not wet.

And then they found that Patter wasn't with them! He seemed to have disappeared completely.

"Gracious! Where's Patter?" said Jane.

"Patter! Patter! Pat!" shouted Jack. But no little puppy came.

"Whistle," said Jane. "I can't whistle properly, Jack, and Benjy can't whistle at all—so you must whistle and whistle."

Jack had a good whistle. He whistled for a long time, then all the children called and called, but still there was no Patter.

"He's lost," said Jane, almost in tears. "Oh, why did we try to cross that marshy ground? I expect Patter didn't want to get his feet wet, so he tried to get round another way, and got lost. Oh, he'll be so miserable and unhappy!"

The children hunted everywhere for Patter, but they couldn't find him. They were very sad. Benjy cried bitterly, for he loved Patter with all his heart.

"It's our fault he's gone!" he said. "We didn't take any notice of him when we were in that marshy field, and now he's gone."

They went home at last, very miserable. Mummy was in the garden, working. She looked surprised when she saw such sad faces.

"What ever is the matter?" she said.

"Oh, Mummy—we did what you said we weren't to do

—we went into the marshy fields and got our feet wet—and we forgot all about Patter," said Jane. "He's lost. Mummy, shall we ever find him again?"

"Poor Patter," said Jack. "We called and we whistled, Mummy, but he didn't come."

"I want Patter," said Benjy, screwing up his face to howl.

Suddenly there was a high little bark and the puppy rushed gaily round the corner of the house! He flung himself on the children, and they went down on their hands and knees and hugged him. He licked their faces over and over again.

"Patter! Where have you been?" they cried.

"He must have been much more obedient and more sensible than you," said Mummy. "He came straight home when he saw you floundering about in the wet fields! I wondered what had happened when I saw him scratching at the front gate."

"Oh, Patter, I *am* glad to see you," said Jane. "How *could* we have forgotten you, even for a moment?"

"Isn't he clever, to know the way home and come all by himself?" said Benjy. "Why, even *I* might get lost, and not know the way home from those fields."

"Well, I'm glad I've got a good dog, even if I've got bad children!" said Mummy, and she laughed.

"Woof!" said Patter, proudly, just as if he understood, and he wagged his tail so fast that it could hardly be seen!

The Kitten and the Cuckoo-Clock

SOMETIMES the children climbed on to one of the walls that ran down the side of the garden, and looked into the one next door.

On one side lived Miss Plum, and Jack said she ought to have a P on the end of her name, and be called Miss Plump, because she was so round and plump and cosy-looking.

She really looked rather nice, but Mummy said she didn't like children, so they mustn't call to Miss Plum, or make too much noise on her side of the garden.

"Why don't some people like children?" said Jane, surprised.

"Well, you see, it's quite likely that the only children those people have known at all well, have been rude, noisy, rough children, with no manners at all," said Mummy. "And of course they don't like *those* boys and girls, and they think that all children must be like them. So they dislike them very much."

"Oh," said Benjy. "Do you suppose she would think we were horrid children too, then, Mummy?"

"She might!" said Mummy. "Anyway, don't bother Miss Plum, please. Let her get used to you, and perhaps she will like you."

"Mummy, I do so wish she *would* like us," said Jane, "because, you know, Miss Plum has got a cuckoo-clock, and I've never seen a cuckoo-clock in my life. Hannah says that when it's twelve o'clock, a little door opens at the top of the clock, and the cuckoo flies out, waves its wings, and calls cuckoo twelve times. Then the cuckoo goes back into the clock and the door shuts."

169

Benjy thought this sounded wonderful. He longed and longed to see the cuckoo in the clock. So did Jane, but Jack laughed. He said he was too old to bother about cuckoos in clocks.

Sometimes Jane and Benjy sat on the wall just when it was what they called "cuckoo-time" which meant something o'clock—two o'clock, or four o'clock or eleven o'clock perhaps—and they heard the cuckoo shouting, "Cuckoo, cuckoo, cuckoo!" inside Miss Plum's house.

"If only we could see it!" sighed Jane.

But they didn't dare to ask Miss Plum, of course. They slid down from the wall as soon as they saw her.

Then one day they saw that Miss Plum had a kitten in her garden! It was such a darling, quite black with four white paws and a white nose. It rushed about all over the place, and chased the bees, and patted every nodding flower-head.

"I wish we could stroke that kitten," said Jane. "Oh, look, Benjy—I do believe it's going to the hole at the bottom of the wall. It may squeeze through!"

It did squeeze through! Then Patter saw it and came pattering up, surprised. He hadn't seen a kitten before. He sniffed at it, and the kitten patted him on the nose.

"Oh, isn't it lovely?" said Jane, and she picked it up. She called to Hannah. "Hannah, do look—the next door kitten has come in!"

"Well, you'd better take it back," said Hannah. "They may miss the little thing."

"Could we have a little play with it first?" said Benjy.

Jane suddenly pulled him away up the garden in excitement. "Benjy! I've got a fine idea! I really have. Let's take the kitten back just about twelve o'clock—and maybe we shall hear and see that cuckoo-clock! We could go in at the garden door, and take the kitten to that room like we've

got, with the glass door. That's the room the cuckoo-clock is in!"

"Oooh, yes," said Benjy. "That door's open to-day, and we could peep in and say: 'Excuse me, Miss Plum, but we've brought back your darling kitten.'"

"It's nearly twelve o'clock now," said Jane. "Quick, let's go. You don't feel afraid, do you, Benjy?"

"No. Not if I'm going with you," said Benjy.

They picked up the kitten, told Patter not to come, and went round to the garden gate next door. They went in and walked round to the back of the house, where the glass door swung open.

Miss Plum was sitting inside, writing. "Please," said Jane, "we've brought your kitten back, it's a darling one!"

Miss Plum looked up and said something, but Jane and

Benjy didn't listen. They were staring in joy at the cuckoo-clock. It was simply lovely.

It was made of carved wood, and there was no glass over the face. Two big hands pointed to the figures. It was just twelve o'clock.

A door above the face flew open suddenly and the children jumped. A wooden bird flew out, with painted blue wings. It flapped them up and down, opened its beak, and the children heard: "Cuckoo! Cuckoo! Cuckoo!" twelve times!

Then the cuckoo shot back, the little door slammed, and there was silence.

"*Oh!*" said Jane, delighted. "How lovely! Miss Plum, aren't you lucky to have that clock to see every day?"

They suddenly remembered that Miss Plum didn't like children, and they said a hurried good-bye and ran home. But they couldn't forget that cuckoo-clock.

They told Jack about it. He was cross that they hadn't let him go too, although he had said he was too old to bother about cuckoo-clocks.

"I know how you can see it!" said Jane. "We can perhaps get the kitten through the hole in the wall again and then *you* can take it back, Jack. You can choose a time just before the cuckoo calls the hour."

So they tempted the kitten through the hole again, by dragging a bit of paper on a string. And, just before three o'clock, Jack carried the tiny thing round to Miss Plum's.

And he saw and heard the cuckoo in the clock. He really thought it was the nicest clock he had ever seen. He rushed

back home as soon as he had heard the cuckoo calling three o'clock.

Then, to Miss Plum's great surprise, the Happy-House children began bringing back her kitten a dozen times a day, always just before the cuckoo flew out of the clock. She didn't know they came because of the clock. She began to think they must like coming to see *her*, and she was pleased.

"It's the first time children have ever seemed to like me enough to come and see me," she thought, and she was glad.

And then the children got a great surprise, for a little note came from Miss Plum, asking them all to go to tea with her the very next day!

Benjy is very Upset

THE children all had their own special jobs to do. Jane had to make her bed and the boys' beds too. She had to dust the two rooms well, and wind the clocks in each room.

Jack had to go any errand his mother wanted, and it was his duty twice a week to go to the farm and fetch the eggs and the butter.

Benjy had to fetch all the waste-paper baskets in the house after breakfast each morning and empty them for Hannah. This was a job he liked doing. There was never anything really exciting in the baskets, but Benjy always hoped there might be.

Once he found a tiny doll in Jane's basket. He looked at it and liked it. "Fancy Jane throwing that dear little doll away!" he thought. "I won't put it into the dustbin. I'll keep it myself, and let it live with my toys on my shelf. Monkey might like it for company."

So he put it beside Monkey in the play-room. Jane saw it there. "Oh, you bad boy," she cried to Benjy, "you've taken my darling little doll! You're not to take my toys."

She snatched the tiny doll away, and knocked Monkey over. "Oh, you've hurt him!" said Benjy. "And I *didn't* take your doll, Jane. You put it in the waste paper basket. You know you did."

"I did *not*!" said Jane, angrily. "As if I would put one of my dolls in the waste-paper basket."

"Well, you did," said Benjy. "You're a naughty story-teller!"

"*You* are, you mean!" said Jane. "You're a bad boy. You took my doll and you told a story about it!"

Benjy began to cry. "Cry-baby!" said Jane. Benjy cried more loudly. Mummy came in to see if he had hurt himself.

"He took my little doll, and he told a naughty story about it," said Jane. "He said I put it into the waste-paper basket."

"Well, she did, she did," sobbed Benjy.

"Darling, I don't think Jane would ever put any of her dolls into the basket," said Mummy.

Benjy ran out of the room, crying as if his heart would break. To think that even Mummy didn't believe him! He went to the stream, and crouched over it. His tears fell into the water and made little plops.

"I'm raining," said Benjy. "I'm raining into the stream. I'll rain some more."

But when he tried, he couldn't. His tears dried up, and he sat back. He felt very hurt and very angry. He *had* found that doll in the basket. Jane and Mummy should have believed him. He always told the truth.

He stayed out there by the stream all morning. He wouldn't come when anybody called him. Nobody knew where he was.

Jane went upstairs with her waste-paper basket, and her little doll. She put the basket beside her little dressing-table, and sat the doll on the table, where she always sat. Then she dusted the room well, and went downstairs to play.

Mummy went up to Jane's room later on to see that she had done it properly. Mummy wouldn't let anything be done badly. If it was done badly it had to be done all over again.

She looked round the room. Yes, Jane had done it very

well. Good little Jane! Mummy could always trust her to do her jobs well.

She was just going out of the room when she happened to look into the waste-paper basket. And to her great surprise, she saw the little doll lying at the bottom of it!

"Well!" said Mummy. "What a queer thing! Surely Jane *hasn't* put it in her waste-paper basket!"

She took out the doll and put it back on the dressing-table. Just at that moment the wind blew. The curtain billowed into the room, and knocked the little doll off the table. It fell into the basket below!

"There now!" said Mummy. "That's what must have happened before! The wind knocked the doll over. Benjy was telling the truth when he said he found Jane's doll in the basket! Poor little Benjy! I didn't believe him and Jane was so cross with him."

She went downstairs and told Jane what she had seen. Jane went very red. Oh dear—how she had scolded poor Benjy. Of course if he had found the doll in the basket, he must at once have thought it had been thrown away—so he had kept it for Monkey.

Jane rushed upstairs and got the doll. She rushed downstairs, almost knocking Patter over in her hurry. He ran at her heels in wonder. What was all the hurry about?

"Benjy!" yelled Jane. "BEN-JEE! I want you."

There was no answer. Benjy wasn't going to talk to anyone that morning. He wasn't going to go in and have any dinner. In fact, he didn't think he would ever in his life go indoors again, he had such a horrid family!

Mummy came out with a beautiful red ribbon fluttering from her fingers. She called Benjy too.

"Benjy! Benjy dear, I want you."

Still no Benjy came. Jane ran down the garden and saw

Benjy crouching under a bush by the stream. He looked cross and miserable.

"Go away," he said. "I don't like you."

"Oh, Benjy, I've come to say I'm sorry I was so horrid!" cried Jane. "You were quite right, the doll was in the basket—but I didn't put her there. The wind blew the curtain and knocked her into the basket. That's what happened. I'm sorry, Benjy. Look, I've brought you the doll for yourself. You can have her."

Benjy smiled. "I feel better now you're sorry," he said. "I'd like the little doll. She was company for Monkey. You're nice, Jane."

Then Mummy came up with the red ribbon. "See what I've found for Monkey," she said. "Come and put it round his neck, Benjy. He will look fine. I'm so sorry I thought you told a story. I know you always tell the truth."

"Yes, I do," said Benjy, beginning to feel much better. "Mummy, I rained on the water. My tears went plop just like the rain-drops."

"Funny little boy!" said Mummy. "Come in and make Monkey look grand."

So in they went, Benjy all smiles. "It just shows, Mummy, that you mustn't call people horrid names till you're quite certain about things, doesn't it?" said Jane. "Benjy, you can have a very long turn of having Patter on your knee, next time we all nurse him."

"Oooh, I'd like that!" said Benjy. And he certainly did, especially when Patter licked his bare knees till they were quite wet!

Jane and Mummy's Birthday

"IT's Mummy's birthday next week," said Jane. "I've got two shillings saved up. I shall go out to-day and see what I can buy with it."

So out she went—but soon she came back in tears. She had lost her little purse with the two shillings in it.

"I've looked everywhere, simply everywhere," said poor Jane. "Someone must have picked it up. It had my name and address inside. They ought to bring it back."

But nobody brought it back, and Jane was sad about it. "I wouldn't have thought there were such mean people in the world!" she said. "If *I* found somebody's purse *and* money, *and* their address inside, I would take it back that very minute. Mummy, why are some people so horrid?"

"Well, I expect they were not taught these things when they were children," Mummy said. "It is only those boys and girls who learn the right things when they are little that grow up into good men and women. That is why I like to teach you so many things."

Jane didn't know what to do about Mummy's birthday. She would only have one penny before it came. She couldn't possibly ask Mummy for money to buy a present, because that would seem as if Mummy had bought her own present, instead of Jane. So she told Hannah and asked her what she could do.

"Well, now," said Hannah, "this is a very busy time of year for me. I'd be glad of a little help from you, Jane, and what's more, I'll pay you for it. I want to make red currant jelly, and I want ripe red currants picking from the garden, and I want them taken off their stalks."

"Oh, I could easily do that!" said Jane. "Do you want some to-day?"

Hannah did, so Jane went out and picked a big basket full. It took her a long time.

Then she went and sat down at the kitchen table and began to pull off the stalks. "Don't do them with your fingers," said Hannah. "Take a fork and you can get them all off at one stroke then."

Jane didn't stop till she had finished the job. Hannah was very pleased with her. She gave her sixpence.

"Oh, thank you!" said Jane, pleased. "Now if only I can get sixpence more, I can buy Mummy a little red vase I saw in the village shop. I know she would love it."

Hannah must have told Miss Plum that Jane wanted jobs to do, because next time Jane went out into the garden, Miss Plum looked over the wall.

"Jane!" said Miss Plum. "Can you write nicely?"

"Well, I can if I try hard," said Jane. "I can write in ink, you know."

"I wonder if you'd like to copy out one or two notes for me," said Miss Plum. "I have to send out a notice about a Sale of Work, and I'm rather too busy to write them all out myself. I'd be very glad to pay you a penny a note if you'd do them."

"Oh, yes!" said Jane, joyfully. "I'm badly wanting money for Mummy's birthday present, Miss Plum. I'll come over now, if you like. I'll do my very best writing."

The notice wasn't very long. It was this: "A Sale of Work will be held at the Church Hall on Monday, July 21. Please come."

Jane was rather a slow writer, and it took her ten minutes to copy out each note nicely. If she made a mistake she began again. She was too honest to let Miss Plum pay her for a badly-written notice.

She did six by tea-time, and Miss Plum was very pleased. She gave her six brown pennies and Jane put them happily in her pocket.

The next few days Jane earned sevenpence. She weeded a garden bed for Daddy and earned threepence. She washed all Mummy's flower-vases very carefully and earned twopence. She got a penny from Hannah for stirring some raspberry jam to keep it from burning.

Then she got a penny from Miss Plum for taking the notices of the Sale of Work round to a good many people.

She had her Saturday penny too, so she had one shilling and eightpence to spend on Mummy's birthday. She bought the little red vase, and she bought a red comb in a case for eightpence. She was very pleased.

Benjy had bought a shoe-horn because Mummy had

broken hers. Jack had spent five shillings! He had bought
a silver brooch with a tiny pearl in the middle of it. Mummy
thought it was really beautiful. Daddy gave her a new pair of
shoes, and Hannah gave her a new purse for her bag.

"How lucky I am!" said Mummy, as she got ready for her
birthday tea. "I shall wear new shoes and get them on easily
with my shoe-horn. I shall comb my hair with my new comb. I
shall wear my lovely new brooch, and have on the table a dear
little red vase full of flowers. And in my bag I shall have a new
purse for my money."

Miss Plum came to tea, too. Benjy ran to her. "Miss Plum,
have you brought Mummy a birthday present? It's her birthday to-day, you know."

"Well, I *have* brought her one," said Miss Plum. "But I'm
not at all sure if she'll like it."

"Show it to me, first," said Benjy. "I shall know at once if she will like it."

So Miss Plum showed him what she had brought. She had a pretty blue and silver box in her hand, tied up with silver ribbon. Benjy untied the ribbon, took off the lid and looked inside.

"Oh!" he said, "it's a box of little chocolate animals. Oh, look at this horse—and this giraffe—and here's a little lamb. Oh, Miss Plum, I am sure Mummy will like this present. I simply love it myself!"

"Well, I thought if Mummy didn't like it very much you could all share it," said Miss Plum, and she gave it to Mummy.

Mummy loved it, and everyone had an animal by their plates at tea-time. Benjy said he couldn't possibly eat his chocolate horse because it was too beautiful. But he did, of course.

They all had Mummy's birthday cake, the one that Hannah had made. It was such a lovely one.

"You must all wish," said Mummy. "A birthday cake has a bit of magic in it, and wishes may come true if you wish whilst you are eating the first piece."

So they all wished, Miss Plum too, but nobody told their wishes, because if they did they wouldn't come true. Even Patter had a piece of the cake, and Benjy was sure he wished whilst he gobbled it, because he looked so solemn.

"Well, good-bye," said Miss Plum, when Mummy's tea-party was over. "Good-bye, little Happy-House family. I'm so glad I know you. Good-bye!"

"Come again!" said everyone. "Everybody is welcome to Happy-House! So come again."

"Wuff!" said Patter, going to the gate with Miss Plum. "What a nice family I belong to! And what a lucky dog I am!"